DEATH IN BLUE FOLDERS

The front bell of the East Side townhouse chimed discreetly and Justin Trent himself crossed the polished marble foyer to answer the door. If all worked out, his daughter could be well again, beautiful and vibrant, with everything to live for. If not . . .

The bell chimed again and he pushed away the dark memory of his only child's slashed wrists, last year, when she had given up.

He opened up the door to a vaguely familiar young woman. Trent prided himself on his politician's memory for names, but he had to grope for this one. "Sergeant— Childe, is it?"

"Harald," she said in a clear neutural voice. "And it's Lieutenant now, Mr. Trent."

By Margaret Maron

DEATH IN BLUE FOLDERS

MARGARET MARON

BANTAM BOOKS
NEW YORK · TORONTO · LONDON · SYDNEY · AUCKLAND

All of the characters in this book
are fictitious, and any resemblance
to actual persons, living or dead,
is purely coincidental.

*This edition contains the complete text
of the original hardcover edition.*
NOT ONE WORD HAS BEEN OMITTED

DEATH IN BLUE FOLDERS
*A Bantam Crime Line Book / published by arrangement with
the author*

Bantam Edition / February 1992

For Claudia Stephenson Brown,
who gave me life and language

DEATH IN
BLUE FOLDERS

CHAPTER I

By nine o'clock that Thursday night, there was little outward indication that murder had occurred six floors above the busy midtown Manhattan avenue.

The body of Clayton Gladwell, a successful middle-aged lawyer, had been photographed from every angle before being carted away for autopsy; the disarray of his suite had been carefully catalogued. Thanks to a late-working accountant down the hall who had discovered the body shortly after six, the paper fire beside his desk was extinguished before it had a chance to spread. Except for a uniformed officer now on guard by Gladwell's doors and a couple of departmental cars double-parked before the building's glass and marble entrance, visible police presence was almost erased.

The doorman stood alert just outside the building and wished for something intelligent to say, some bit of helpfulness he could offer the tall, slate-eyed police lieutenant who waited silently on the sidewalk for her partner to come down from Gladwell's office.

Her dark hair was braided into a knot at the nape of her slender neck and her summer-weight pantsuit must have been chosen for utility and efficiency because there was certainly nothing stylish about its loose cut or drab beige color. A reserved, austere young woman who neither blamed nor criticized, yet her air of quiet authority reduced the doorman to nervous chatter.

She had already heard his explanations, his justification for not being at the door every moment: how, if people didn't look like bums and looked as if they knew where they were going, no doorman in the world was going to give them the third degree. There were nearly sixty different offices in this building, he explained again, and not just lawyers like Mr. Gladwell but doctors and tax specialists and professionals like that and they all saw clients after five o'clock. Look at all the people still trickling out. Nobody could keep track in the early hours of the evening. After eight or nine, sure—the doors got locked at seven, in fact—but before that? Impossible.

Lieutenant Sigrid Harald nodded and wished that Tillie would hurry.

Detective Tildon was always tempted by papers to sort, and Clayton Gladwell's files had been upended. What wasn't burned had been strewn throughout the suite. The worst of the charred scraps had been carefully transferred to the lab where trained personnel would piece back together as much as possible, but that was only a fraction of the paper on the floor and Tillie'd had a pleased look on his face as he contemplated the mess.

Nevertheless, it had been a hot weary day for both of them and Sigrid thought she'd made it clear that everything could wait until tomorrow morning.

"Be right with you, Lieutenant," he'd promised as she left to question the doorman.

That was twenty minutes ago.

Sigrid looked at her watch again. As a rule, she didn't begrudge overtime, but a deadline was looming in her personal life and she was supposed to view an apartment this evening. Her building was going co-op and she had until August first to buy or move.

The sidewalk beneath her feet radiated with summer's flaming heat, reminding her that it was already mid-July. In two weeks, she could be homeless.

Of course she could always bite the bullet and buy the damned apartment.

Except that she really didn't like it enough to mortgage

her life for the outrageous sum they were asking. So she'd have to keep looking and what was keeping Tillie?

The steady stream of yellow taxis flowing past the building was diverted as one slid to a stop by the double-parked police cars, temporarily triple-parking in front of Sigrid and the doorman. Impatient horns cursed the delay while four lanes of traffic squeezed into two. Idly she watched a woman emerge from the cab's darkness, hand the exact change to the driver and come toward them.

"Tch-tch," clicked the doorman and advanced to meet her.

"Sorry, Nellie," Sigrid heard him say, "but you won't be able to get in tonight. Mr. Gladwell's been shot. He's dead."

The woman's faded green dress hung loosely on her large, amply fleshed frame. Her wiry gray hair was short and brushed away from a strong forehead, and Sigrid's trained eyes put her age at late fifties, perhaps early sixties, even though the woman's face held few wrinkles. Her dress was shabby and her large feet wore loafers with run-down heels, yet her rawboned hands clutched a good-quality leather handbag as she stood wordlessly before the solicitous doorman.

"I'll get you another cab," he said; but Sigrid stepped forward.

"Did you have an appointment with Clayton Gladwell?" she called.

The woman looked mutely from Sigrid to the doorman.

"That's Lieutenant Harald," he told her. "From the police. Homicide." He brought her over to Sigrid. "This is Nellie Goldenweiser," he said. "She cleans for Mr. Gladwell a couple of times a month."

"Gladwell's office was only cleaned twice a month?" asked Sigrid.

At the moment the dead attorney's rooms were admittedly a mess, what with all his papers strewn around, the abortive fire smothered by a fire extinguisher, and so many people tramping in and out; but that had seemed a superficial and temporary slovenliness imposed on basically well-kept quarters.

"Our regular crew cleans every night," the doorman

said quickly, sensing criticism. "Nellie's like extra. Mr. Gladwell was very particular."

"I polish the wood," said the woman. "Oil the leather, stuff like that. Things the night people don't have time for." Her voice was unexpectedly husky. "If he's dead, I guess I'll go take my oils and cloths."

"I'm sorry, Mrs. Goldenweiser," said Sigrid, "but nothing can be removed from the premises until we complete our investigation."

"So what's to investigate about furniture oils and polishing cloths? And it's Miss not Missus," she told Detective Tildon, who had finally arrived on the sidewalk and was now writing the woman's name in his notebook.

She spelled it out for him and gave an address over in Bensonhurst. From south Brooklyn to midtown Manhattan seemed like an expensive cab ride for a cleaning woman, thought Sigrid, but her knowledge of the other boroughs was hazy and perhaps Miss Goldenweiser had only ridden from the nearest subway stop. Judging from her shoes, her feet must give her problems and she probably found even short walks uncomfortable.

"We won't keep you tonight," said Tillie, "but someone will be out to talk to you tomorrow or the next day."

"What's to talk?" asked the woman. Her husky voice dropped into a rasping growl. "You think Mr. Gladwell and me was friends? Took tea together? He needed somebody to polish his wood, I needed the money."

"You didn't like him?" asked Sigrid.

Miss Goldenweiser's dark brown eyes studied the police officer's thin face for a long moment, then she shrugged. "Like-schmike, it's a job. Now I gotta find another one."

They let her go then. She refused the doorman's offer to hail a cab, and as she shuffled away from them in runover loafers, the streetlights overhead cast her shadowed form into a caricatured symbol of all the cleaning women in the world—women alone, existing on minimum wages, but undefeated.

"Nellie's getting old," said the doorman, made reflective by the droop in the woman's shoulders as she receded. "Funny how you go along and people are the same as when you first saw them and then one day you look up and they're old."

Sigrid Harald pulled herself away from sidewalk philosophy and moved over to the curb and the unmarked patrol car they'd arrived in earlier. The day had been long and hot, and she was tired enough to lean against the car's solid bulk while Tillie used the top as a desk, but her voice was still brisk as she addressed the few loose ends at hand. With one eye on her watch and the other on Tillie's pen racing across his notebook page, she laid out the next day's schedule, reports she wanted pushed, people she wanted to see.

"I suppose we ought to start with Gladwell's secretary or his assistant, if he had one," she said.

"Office manager. Nancy Kuipers. She called right after you left. That was what took me so long," Tillie said in oblique apology. "She wanted to come right over, but I put her off till morning."

He pocketed the notebook and opened the car door. "Drop you somewhere?"

She shook her head. "I'm going uptown. West side."

As Tillie fitted the key in the ignition, he suddenly remembered something and flung open the door to call, "Hey, Lieutenant!" But she was too far away and going in the opposite direction from which the car was headed.

Tillie shrugged and got back in. The way she'd kept checking her watch—a date perhaps? He tried to imagine his reserved lieutenant in an emotional relationship, her thin body clothed in something lacy and flowing. The image was difficult to conjure. She probably went to buttoned-up philatelic lectures with someone as dry as old stamp albums.

And as for what he'd forgotten—well, tomorrow was soon enough for her to learn that Gladwell had possessed photocopies of FBI reports.

CHAPTER II

Lieutenant Harald's long strides quickly covered the two blocks from Gladwell's office to the subway stop. She descended dirty steps, and a musty cavelike odor of warm damp concrete met her as she fished a token from her pocket and pushed through the turnstile.

At this hour the platforms on both sides of the tracks were fairly peopled, and while she waited the police-woman idly scanned the area for Miss Goldenweiser's faded green dress. There was no sign of the cleaning woman even though the IRT was the most direct train from here back to Brooklyn.

Unless she'd taken another cab?

With a shriek of metal against metal, an uptown train braked into the station and Sigrid Harald dismissed Miss Goldenweiser and that woman's commuting arrangements from her mind.

A couple of changes later, Sigrid came up onto the well-lit sidewalks of Central Park West and immediately located the coffee shop Roman had specified.

"Sorry," she said, sliding into the booth where a glass of iced coffee, melted now, waited for her on the narrow plastic table across from a reproachful Roman Tramegra. "We had to go over to Jersey this afternoon, it was late when we got back, and then there was a new case we had to look into."

"Something interesting?" Tramegra asked hopefully.

Roman Tramegra was an unexpected emergence into her life. Rescued by her mother from some sort of complications in Sicily this spring, the large soft man had receding sandy hair, hooded eyes and a full-toned bass voice that spoke a pompous mixture of cinema British and educated Midwest.

Anne Harald was a photojournalist whose assignments had kept her out of the country for the last few months, and in her mother's absence Sigrid found herself feeling vaguely responsible for Tramegra. When circumstances drove him from the apartment Anne had lent him, Sigrid had reluctantly allowed him the use of her own tiny guest room.

She was a solitary person and lived alone by choice, but since she'd already received the co-op notice from her apartment building's management, and since Roman had promised to find her a new apartment in return for this emergency haven, she knew the arrangement would soon die a natural death.

In the meantime, having a roommate was working out better than she'd expected. If he'd smothered her with attention it would have been unbearable; fortunately there was a certain amount of reserve in Roman's manner. He was tactful about her need for privacy and seemed to know when to leave her alone. Although not that much older than she, he treated her rather as an elderly uncle might treat his schoolboy nephew—kindly, but not terribly involved—so the novelty of coming home to someone hadn't yet worn thin.

Too, her dinners had previously been grilled cheese sandwiches, canned soup, or cartons of something from the corner delicatessen. Roman Tramegra's concoctions weren't always better but, just as a tone-deaf singer will occasionally hit some of a song's right notes, so his meals occasionally contained something both interesting and edible. She was learning verbal tact, she told herself, a useful skill for someone on the public payroll.

She was also learning to deflect his magpie interest in her work. Tramegra supplemented his small private income with piecemeal freelance writing. Anything that caught his attention could be turned into a couple of paragraphs or a short article for some of the lesser-paying magazines and newspapers. His latest sale had been to a children's monthly, an article on raising butterfly caterpillars as pets, but he still harbored the notion that he could write a best-selling thriller if Sigrid would only cooperate. Surely she had worked on homicide cases more exciting than the routine shootings, bludgeonings and poisonings she'd let drop so far?

Thus his look of eagerness at the mention of a new case.

"No locked rooms, no pygmy dart guns," she said, then took pity on his deflated look. "There is one puzzling thing though: the victim was a lawyer and whoever shot him seems to have dumped some of his files into a large metal waste can and set them on fire."

It wasn't enough to divert him. "The killer's probably someone in the building who wanted to destroy blackmail evidence without the inconvenience of moving to new quarters," he said airily. "Which reminds me, my dear— we are quite late. Never mind. Perhaps the people who were due to look at ten were late as well."

They weren't.

When Sigrid and Roman arrived at the apartment on the sixteenth floor of a nearby building, they found another couple with the rental agent. If the young husband and wife were hesitant before, seeing potential rivals sealed their decision to take the apartment.

"It's farther uptown than I wanted to be, but isn't the view just super?" enthused the girl.

Sigrid smiled politely and joined her at a window overlooking Central Park. Greenery and scenery seldom moved her, but she had to admit that the night view of the park was very pretty with lights reflecting on the reservoir and, yes, beyond the trees the lighted buildings along Fifth and Madison avenues were indeed quite beautiful. For a moment she almost regretted missing out on this view, then common sense made her look at the scarred plaster and the exposed pipes in the tiny bath and kitchenette. And while she certainly didn't plan to house a steady string of guests such as her mother encouraged, she did like extra space and here there was only one large room for eating, sleeping, and entertaining.

In fact, the young woman was already deep in a discussion with her husband about camouflaging their bed with bolsters and throws to look like a living room couch by day.

Roman was gloomy as they rode down in the elevator. "We're never going to have any luck unless we start arriving first," he observed.

This was the third appointment to view for which she'd been late, so Sigrid couldn't blame him for criticizing. Disliking tardiness in others, she tried to be punctual herself; but lately her caseload was so heavy that schedules had become a sometime thing. She'd cleared the paperwork on four cases today, though, so . . .

"I'll try to do better," she promised and they made the subway ride downtown in companionable silence.

The telephone was ringing and a cloud of acrid fumes met them as Sigrid unlocked the apartment door.

"My casserole!" Roman exclaimed. "My wonderful curried cauliflower casserole!"

He dashed past her to the kitchen and Sigrid mentally crossed her fingers that he would be too late. Curried cauliflower didn't top the list of foods she looked forward to. Since flames weren't actually pouring from the kitchen, she answered the telephone.

"Where the hell have you been all evening?" asked an annoyed male voice. "I thought you were working days and if you are, why can't that late-blooming flower child you took in ever—"

The rest was lost in a clatter of lids and exhaust fan. Sigrid closed the door to the kitchen and waited.

"You there?" asked Oscar Nauman.

"I'm here," she said coldly. "Did you call to complain

about my lack of answering service or did you have something to say?"

"You can dance, can't you? Waltz, foxtrot, that sort of thing?"

Recalling childhood dancing class with white gloves and black patent-leather Mary Janes, Sigrid agreed that she could waltz and foxtrot and that sort of thing.

"With that proper Southern grandmother of yours, I thought you'd probably know something earlier than the funky chicken."

"Actually, it was my great-uncle in Brooklyn who took me to dancing classes," Sigrid said. "Uncle Lars."

He brushed the clarification aside. "What about a long dress?"

"No."

"No, you don't have one? Or no, you won't wear it?"

"Both. Listen, Nauman, it's too late in the evening for Twenty Questions. I don't think I'm going to like the point, but would you please get to it?"

"There's a ball Saturday night to benefit MOMA. I'm supposed to be one of the drawing cards."

A logical choice, she thought, considering that Oscar Nauman was one of the country's leading abstract artists. His paintings hung in every important modern collection, including that of the Museum of Modern Art; so, yes, there were those who would buy an expensive tax-deductible ticket for the chance to meet him.

She herself had met him this spring after a murder in the Vanderlyn College art department, where he was chairman. She supposed she should be flattered by his invitation.

"And you expect me to go to a formal ball with you on two days' notice?" Her voice wasn't angry, just curious.

"They asked me back in the spring. That was just after Riley was killed," he reminded her. "It was easier to say yes than fight, and then I just forgot all about it until they sent the tickets over today."

"No," said Sigrid.

"You'll enjoy it," he said, ignoring her refusal. "It'll

be good for your career. You can rub shoulders with the mayor. Ask him for a raise."

Sigrid smiled. "No."

He heard the smile in her voice. "I'm a damn good dancer, Siga."

She thought about dancing with this man who raised such ambivalent emotions inside her. About waltzing. The dress might be a nuisance, but moving to formal music with a good dancer was almost like swimming in another dimension.

"What time?" she asked.

CHAPTER III

∎

Routine procedures had kept the police guard from letting anyone enter before the lieutenant arrived, so an impatient cluster of people waited before Clayton Gladwell's office the next morning. As Sigrid and Tillie emerged from the elevator and came down the hall, one of the women stepped forward to meet them.

She was a small, intense redhead, early forties, and her trim figure was enhanced by a shape-fitting green linen suit. Her skin had the delicate translucence of many auburn-haired women, but there were faint lines around her mouth and her green eyes were red-rimmed though her emotions seemed under control when she introduced herself.

"I'm Nancy Kuipers, Lieutenant, Mr. Gladwell's office manager. Look—there's so much to be done. We've got to get in."

"Of course." Sigrid motioned for the guard to unseal the doors. "But for the moment, please stay in the reception area until we decide where to begin."

"Good lord!" exclaimed a young blonde who had entered first and now stood rooted at the front desk, appalled by the ransacking. "What a bloody awful mess!"

The Gladwell suite was eclectic contemporary: pale blue walls with lots of carved white molding, gleaming parquet floors, oriental-inspired carpets of muted blues and golds on a cream background, comfortable sofas covered in shantung, and mellow wooden pieces effectively placed.

The receptionist's desk, a delicate Queen Anne lowboy, had its drawers agape; beyond it and to the left, down the wide hall that led to Gladwell's office, a blizzard of paper covered the carpets. Through far double doors opening into Gladwell's office, more of the same could be seen. Acrid smells of melted plastic and burned paper lingered in the air, although they were rapidly being displaced by the receptionist's expensive perfume.

The pale blue telephone console on the lowboy-cum-desk chimed melodiously. The blonde touched a lighted button and in clipped British accents said, "Good morning. Clayton Gladwell, Attorney at Law . . . yes? . . . yes, we were all quite shocked. No, I'm sorry, sir, but Mrs. Kuipers is presently engaged. Thank you for calling, sir."

She looked at Nancy Kuipers and said, "Old Mr. Ferguson. He just read about it in the morning paper and wanted to express condolences."

On the previous evening Sigrid had noticed a small conference room adjoining the reception area, and now she and Tillie shepherded the three women and lone man inside. As they took places around the oval mahogany table, Mrs. Kuipers introduced each by name and title.

The pretty blond receptionist was Millicent Barr. Intelligence flashed in her Wedgwood-blue eyes and her smile was friendly as she acknowledged the introduction.

"Miss Barr's been with us about a year now, isn't it, Milly?"

"Fourteen months," the girl said. In another year she would be totally cool and elegantly chic, but at the present she was still working at it and an appealing adolescence kept popping through the thin patina of sophistication. She couldn't be more than twenty and Sigrid wasn't surprised to hear that this was her first position, that she'd been hired straight off an airplane from England.

It was her job to answer and reroute telephone calls,

greet clients, help whenever extra typing piled up, and read proof on many of the legal papers which passed through the office. Sigrid suspected she'd been chosen originally because she was so extraordinarily pretty and because her fair coloring matched the decor. Her intelligence was a bonus.

Beside her sat Jean Parrish, Gladwell's secretary. She was several years older and several pounds heavier than Millicent Barr and her once-fair hair had darkened to a dull brown, but she seemed unaware of the unflattering contrast between the Barr girl and herself. If anything, a vacant expression in her eyes made her look slightly bored.

Not so Dan Embry, who sat across from her. Gladwell's law clerk wore rimless glasses and his eyes were bright and interested behind those thick lenses. Short and chubby with fringed white hair half-circling an otherwise shiny pink scalp, Embry was probably around seventy. According to Mrs. Kuipers, he was semiretired and worked there only two or three mornings a week unless Gladwell was preparing a complicated contract or trust and needed Embry to look up precedents. He had left at lunchtime the day before; Kuipers had worked through lunch and taken off early at two. Milly Barr guiltily admitted that without her presence, she and Jean Parrish might have left a few minutes before five.

"I buzzed Mr. G. around 4:30 and he said he had some work he wanted to finish but Jean and I could go ahead and lock up."

Pressed for the specific time, Jean Parrish looked blank, but Milly thought they'd rung for the elevator about 4:45. Both agreed there had been nothing out of the ordinary in Gladwell's manner.

"You don't have to stay today, Dan," said Nancy Kuipers. "There's no point in continuing with that infringement now."

"Nonsense, Nancy," he said briskly. "I shall certainly stay and help sort papers. Good grief, girl! Didn't you take a good look? It's enough to keep the lot of us busy for days."

"Thank you, Dan," she said and took a deep breath

to steady her suddenly tremulous voice before turning back to Sigrid. "There's one more member of the staff, Lieutenant. A quasi-member, actually. Bailey Dunne. He's a private investigator who does—*did*—Mr. Gladwell's fieldwork."

"Was there much?" asked Sigrid. "I had the impression that Mr. Gladwell didn't handle criminal cases."

"As a rule, he didn't," agreed Mrs. Kuipers. "Most of his practice was limited to civil law—deeds and wills, trusts and contracts—but occasionally these did entail some investigative backup. Mr. Gladwell liked having someone available on short notice even though there wasn't enough work to employ someone full-time."

Mrs. Kuipers still wore a look of numbness, but her voice was businesslike as she described Clayton Gladwell's arrangements with Bailey Dunne. In lieu of a full-time salary, Gladwell had given Dunne and his predecessors the use of an office on the other side of the reception room, telephone privileges, limited secretarial services, and separate pay for each job performed. He stipulated that he would have first call on the investigator's time, but otherwise the man would be his own boss, at liberty to free-lance.

"It's a very equitable arrangement, but I'm afraid most PI's didn't seem to think so. Mr. Dunne's been with us about two months, but most don't last beyond six months to a year."

"Is he around now?" asked Tillie.

Mrs. Kuipers shook her head. "Chicago, I think. Milly?"

"Flew out yesterday morning," the receptionist confirmed. "Due back in tomorrow night."

"And there you have one of the reasons they don't last long," said the office manager. "Mr. Gladwell required them to file an itinerary whenever they left the city in case he needed them on short notice. Most investigators resented it."

During this, the telephone kept chiming at ever more frequent intervals as clients heard the news of the attorney's death and called to express shock and concern. Miss Barr had been back and forth so many times that she no longer sat down at the mahogany conference table, just hovered in the doorway.

"One moment, Miss Barr, and then you may remain at your desk," said Sigrid. "We'll be speaking to each of you separately again, but for now, does anyone know if Mr. Gladwell had a particular enemy? Had he been threatened? Perhaps antagonized someone recently?"

There were frowns of concentration and murmured negatives from the four.

"It wasn't that sort of practice," said Mrs. Kuipers.

"From the state of this office," Sigrid continued, "it would seem that the killer might have been looking for a particular document, some special piece of paper. That implies a client or possibly someone close enough to a client to think that the document was in Mr. Gladwell's possession. Does this suggest anything to any of you?"

Once more the shaking of heads.

The telephone chimed again, but Sigrid compelled Millicent Barr's presence for a final word. "Think about it, please. All of you. And let us know if you remember any person or any incident, however trivial, that can help us determine Mr. Gladwell's killer."

Released, Milly Barr scampered across the cream-and-blue carpets; the others stirred and rose hesitantly when Sigrid stood.

"It's just a formality," she said, "but Detective Tildon will need to know where each of you was last night. Mrs. Parrish, if you and Mr. Embry will let him start with you two, Mrs. Kuipers and I will begin outside."

As Sigrid and the office manager crossed the reception area, Milly Barr pressed the hold button on her console and said, "It's Justin Trent."

Mrs. Kuipers shook her head. "Hold all calls, Milly, and tell everyone I'll be in touch as soon as possible."

"I told him that, but he's most insistent, Mrs. Kuipers."

Resigned, the older woman took the receiver, identified herself and listened intently. Sigrid watched her expression turn to puzzled surprise.

"If Mr. Gladwell said he had finished all negotiations

and arrangements, Mr. Trent, then I'm sure he had.
One moment, please."

She covered the mouthpiece and said, "Milly, did you
arrange for a Miss Elsner to fly in from L.A.?"

The girl nodded, pulled her daybook forward and
pointed to a memo written the afternoon before.

Again Mrs. Kuipers spoke into the telephone. "Mr.
Trent, I was out of the office yesterday afternoon so I
wasn't aware everything was coming to a head so quickly.
Reservations were made for one adult and one child in
the name of Rachel Elsner. The flight gets into Kennedy
this evening at six-twenty." She read a further notation
to which Milly Barr was pointing. "And we've booked
her a room at the Waldorf. Assuming the plane is on
schedule, I'll meet them and you can expect us, shall we
say, around eight . . . Your check?"

Her eyes queried Milly Barr, who murmured, "I de-
posited it on the way home."

"No, Mr. Trent, it's safe. You won't need to issue a
duplicate and we'll be in touch about the balance . . .
goodbye."

Her green eyes brimmed with tears as she returned
the receiver to the Barr girl. "It's so damned unfair! Clay
worked so hard for this and now he isn't here to see it!"

The receptionist's eyes filled, too. She pulled a flat
box of tissues from her desk drawer and offered them to
Nancy Kuipers, who blew briskly and then forced herself
to face the situation at hand.

"I suppose you'll want my alibi as well, Lieutenant?"
she asked. "My daughter's ballet class had a recital at
four and Mr. Gladwell insisted I take the whole afternoon
off. She and I went out to dinner afterwards to celebrate.
Sing Wu's down on Second Avenue. It wasn't crowded
and we go there often enough that I think they'll remember us."

Her voice was so brittle that the words fell like bits
of broken glass. "We were home by seven and—Oh,
God! I don't even know when it happened!"

"We think around five-thirty," Sigrid said.

The woman's tears made her uncomfortable and she

led the way down the littered hall toward Gladwell's office.

On the right was Nancy Kuipers's office. The pale blue walls prevalent in the rest of the suite gave way here to pale green, and the forest green suede on the executive chair behind the desk also seemed chosen in deference to the office manager's auburn hair. The desk drawers had been plundered, but otherwise, the hurricane seemed to have skipped this office.

Opposite her door, an archway opened into a large double room divided by a runner of the same blue-and-cream pattern as in the rest of the suite. To the left, white wooden shelves covered all three walls from floor to ceiling and were filled with leatherbound law books. In the center stood a long walnut library table and several leather chairs.

On the right, a bank of low white file cabinets lined the other three walls to form a horseshoe around Jean Parrish's desk. The utilitarian area was normally softened by flowering plants and gilt-framed landscapes on the pale blue walls, but it was here that the intruder had created the greatest chaos. Every single file drawer had been methodically emptied upon the desk until papers and manila folders slid to the floor, piled up in drifts, and overflowed toward the law library. From there they seemed to have been kicked into the main hall.

Released by Detective Tildon, Jean Parrish joined them at her desk. "Can I start now?" she asked. She appeared surprisingly unannoyed by the colossal mess.

Kuipers looked at Sigrid, who nodded and said, "I know I'm probably asking the impossible, but as you go along, try to remember if anything obvious is missing from any of those folders."

Mrs. Parrish shrugged. "I'll try, but I don't have a very good memory for things like that. Everything's so much alike, you know?"

They left her sorting papers and moved on down the hall. Next on the right was a staff lounge with coffee maker, electric teapot and the usual accessories on a neatly kept counter beside comfortable lounge chairs. There was no disorder here.

Beyond that, the main hall terminated at the double doors into Gladwell's private office. To the left, a narrower passageway led to an outer door and a public hall that went to the building's rear elevators.

"That door was found open by the accountant who reported Mr. Gladwell's murder," Sigrid said. "He smelled smoke a little before six and came along the hall. The rear door to the inner office was also ajar. When he entered, he found Mr. Gladwell slumped over his desk and a paper fire smoldering in his wastebasket. He extinguished the fire and then called us."

Mrs. Kuipers approached her dead employer's desk. "The blue files!" she said. "Why would they burn the blue files? And where—?"

She circled the desk and answered her own question. The lower drawer of Gladwell's desk was closed, but a set of keys dangled from the lock.

CHAPTER IV

I

It was the first time the different folder colors had registered with Sigrid, but now she recalled that most of the files littering the office suite were a creamy tint, while the singed remans found in Gladwell's wastebasket were pale blue.

"Was there something special about blue folders?" she asked.

"Only to Clay," said Nancy Kuipers. "They were his personal favorites, the offbeat things he did most of the investigation for himself. I guess that's why he kept them locked in his desk. Most of his practice was rather dry, but occasionally there'd be something with an interesting twist and Clay would go all cloak-and-daggerish."

Her tone was indulgent as if she were remembering a boyish side to Gladwell that the rest of the world had seldom seen.

"He wouldn't even let me see more than was absolutely necessary because some of the material was sensitive. Not that he didn't trust me," she added quickly, "but Clay had trained himself not to take risks with someone else's privacy. Especially since some of the people are celebrities—people the newspapers love to write about."

"People like Justin Trent?" asked Sigrid. She had been

surprised to hear his name before. If asked, she would have thought that a man as wealthy as Justin Trent, a man whose financial interests were global, whose opinions were listened to by presidents and senators—surely such a man would be represented by a much larger firm.

"This was definitely a blue folder. It's so exciting!" said Nancy Kuipers. Even in her grief, she could be uplifted by the thought of what Gladwell had accomplished. "You mustn't say a word about it yet—it'll be splashed all over the newspapers and television soon enough—but Clay has found his grandson!"

Sigrid was startled. "Jamie Logan? Are you sure?"

It was almost as incredible as hearing that the Lindbergh baby had been found alive and well, but Mrs. Kuipers was certain.

"Mr. Trent hired Clay to find the boy as soon as the FBI gave up on it. For three years Clay's been chasing leads all over the U.S., and last month he finally found him. It was exactly as the FBI thought—the girl who took him had just lost her own baby and wanted a child to replace it. She died this spring and her sister's been keeping him ever since."

"Rachel Elsner?" asked Sigrid, remembering the telephone conversation a few minutes ago.

Kuipers nodded. "She still has no idea who he really is, but she never believed he was her sister's child. Bailey Dunne finished checking all the details last week. Dave Shovener—he was our P.I. before Dunne—picked up the girl's trail in the Bronx and talked to the people who were there four years ago and who remembered that she'd moved on right after her baby died. Bailey found her sister in California, then Clay arranged for blood tests and the types match—it's him! Won't it be wonderful for them? That poor woman. She had a nervous breakdown after the kidnapping, you know.

"Oh, damn it all! This was going to be the crowning touch to Clay's career and now—"

"Crowning touch?" asked Sigrid, looking beyond the sensational news of Jamie Logan's return.

"Clay was retiring. He had a bad heart and the doctors told him he'd be dead in two years if he didn't slow down. That's when he decided he wouldn't just slow down, he'd quit."

A delicate flush suffused Nancy Kuipers's cheeks and made her look younger, more vulnerable.

"We were going to marry," she said softly. "He planned to have everything cleared away by Labor Day. We were going to fly to Nice and be married there. He said it was the most wonderful place in the world to retire to." Her small hands clenched in convulsive fists. "Have you ever been in France?" she asked abruptly.

Sigrid nodded.

"I've never been out of the state except to Florida once." Her voice went tremulous again and Sigrid, who was always ill at ease with raw emotion, began to question her about the blue folders.

"I think he used to have about a dozen," said Kuipers, grateful for the move to less sensitive ground. She sorted the smoke-stained documents and spread four or five remaining blue folders on Gladwell's desk.

"I had so little to do with these that I forget most of the details. I think one was about passports and documenting someone's citizenship papers and there were a couple of missing heirs like this one."

Sigrid read the label on the folder she'd opened: *Helmut Dussel*. A letter was stapled to the inside left cover. The ornate letterhead was of a West German bank and described a former Austrian citizen last known to be in the New York area. It seemed that Helmut Dussel was one of the beneficiaries under a 1950 trust that was finally being distributed, and the bank was retaining Gladwell to find him.

"That was about six years ago." Kuipers shuffled through the crumpled scorched papers until she found several that pertained to Dussel.

"Clay found him in a nursing home up in Queens," she said. "He was past seventy and had used up almost all his savings. Thanks to Clay, he's having a decent old age."

Sigrid recognized the name on another label. "Elena Dorato?" she asked. "The actress?"

Kuipers frowned. "I'm not really sure why he had that one."

She opened it, changed her mind, and slid that folder under Dussel's. When Sigrid reached for it, she started to resist, then shrugged and handed it over.

Inside were photocopies of densely typed pages. Pages that carried a stamped security rating.

"Why, these are FBI reports," Sigrid said.

The small woman looked at Sigrid defiantly. "It was only for his own private use. He was a Dorato fan. Besides, he had a right to see them."

"Gladwell was once an FBI agent?"

"For about five years after he got out of law school. Then he decided that he preferred private practice and resigned."

"And brought along some keepsakes?" asked the policewoman.

Kuipers flushed at the implied censure, but said nothing as Sigrid skimmed through the reports of Elena Dorato's drowning.

Elena Dorato. The Golden Elena.

She'd been a teenage film star of the late forties and early fifties. She was golden-haired and golden-voiced, and her most famous film was *Cinderella*, a magical retelling of the fairy tale that had made it hers forever. It was innocence and gaiety spangled with musical stardust. Blending animation and real life, it had become a cult film and still drew a major share of the ratings whenever it was shown on television. The delightful "Dance of the Enchanted Mice" became a first recital piece for beginning ballet students all across the country and Elena Dorato's wistful "When Love Lies in Ashes" was an immediate classic. Many singers recorded it, but her version outsold the rest ten to one, so identified with her as it was.

Cinderella had been a once-in-a-lifetime coalescence of perfect script, music and cast. None of Dorato's later movies actually lost money, but neither did any of them ever come close to matching that spectacular success.

There were unhappy love affairs, rumors of drugs and

drink, and a dimming of her youthful radiance that made her turn reclusive.

In the early sixties, past thirty, the golden tones of her voice darkening, Elena Dorato had sailed for Italy to star in a serious film drama that was expected to give her career new impetus. The ship, ironically named the *Golden Princess*, was four nights out from New York when Elena Dorato abruptly disappeared from her first-class cabin.

Because her disappearance involved a U.S. vessel on the high seas, the FBI entered the case immediately, probably spurred on by J. Edgar Hoover himself, who was known to own a copy of *Cinderella* and who had been a devout fan of Elena Dorato.

The *Golden Princess* had been searched from stern to bow, every passenger and every crew member thoroughly questioned, and all Dorato's movements aboard carefully reconstructed.

Now in Clayton Gladwell's office, Lieutenant Sigrid Harald scanned the Bureau's summarized field reports which were attached to the passenger and crew lists. Even though couched in official language, the reports made interesting reading: how Elena Dorato had remained in her cabin most of the time, emerging only for a late-night turn around the deck each evening followed by the midnight buffet in the Moonglow Lounge.

Dressed in gold lamé and topazes, she had eaten caviar and sipped quinine water, but those who spoke with her thought she had seemed depressed and edgy.

An elderly Frenchman heard a splash shortly after 2 A.M. that last evening and gave the alarm. The ship immediately executed a Williamson Turn and steamed back along its own wake while a hasty head count revealed that one passenger was indeed missing—Elena Dorato.

Her cabin was unlocked and on her dressing table they found a note in her handwriting: *Forgive me. I cannot be Ingrid Bergman.* It was speculated later that she'd realized she couldn't make the transition from light romantic lead to serious dramatic character actress.

She had traveled alone, sending her maid ahead to

Rome by plane. All her jewels were left untouched in their cases and none of the passengers seemed to have any personal connection with the actress, so foul play had been ruled out.

An abstract of her will was appended to the report. Childless and lacking close relatives, Dorato had redrawn the document a week before she sailed, further proof that she'd planned to end her life. Half her large estate was split between an actors' relief fund and a film industry retirement home; the other half went to various annuities for a long list of dressers, maids, housekeepers and cooks who had served her through the years.

The report concluded that Elena Dorato had committed suicide of her own free will.

Sigrid looked at the photograph clipped to the back of the blue folder. It was a studio publicity still and showed a young Elena Dorato at the moment her Cinderella rags were being transformed into a gauzy ball gown, her lovely face captured forever in a moment of delighted wonder.

Sigrid closed the folder without comment and reached for the next. It was labeled *Bhattacherjea, Drs. Morarji and Ishrad* and had suffered extensively from the fire. With difficulty, Sigrid made out the name of an East Side hospital with which the Bhattacherjeas seemed to have a connection. From the charred scraps that remained, it appeared that Gladwell had handled a visa change for them, something about a niece's expired visitor's visa being changed to a student visa.

"That was more or less a personal favor," said Nancy Kuipers. "Dr. Morarji Bhattacherjea was the radiologist who did the X rays and fluoroscopes when Clay's heart condition was discovered this spring.

"The little girl was his wife's niece—I believe she's an anesthesiologist. There was some mix-up about the child's papers. They were getting the runaround down at Immigration and Clay was able to cut through some of the red tape for them."

The last of the blue files was labeled *Penelope Naughton*.

"Is she still alive?" asked Sigrid. It was a name from

New York's glittering past, a name synonymous with the old Algonquin Round Table and the brittle sophisticates who had set the tone of the twenties and thirties.

By day, Penelope Naughton had written frothy novels which, though lighter than champagne bubbles, nevertheless sold as briskly as what was passing for champagne in those days. By night, she helped the roaring twenties roar. If acidulous caricaturists were too fond of emphasizing her prominent nose, at least they paid full tribute to her copper hair and truly superb legs.

Besides, New York had been rife with empty-headed beauties, but only one Naughty Penny. Outrageous repartee and brilliant retorts had fallen from her lips like newly minted coppers that were collected and circulated as coins of the realm. "As bright as a new Penny" had been the supreme accolade for anyone else's clever witticism.

Nor were all her antics strictly verbal. Now-respectable octogenarians could still evoke a nostalgic chuckle from their contemporaries by recalling with a wink and a nudge "that night in Sardi's when a bad Penny turned *up!*"

Then, in the mid-thirties, as abruptly as Garbo had quit making films, Penelope Naughton disappeared from the New York scene. Her books never went completely out of print—every ten or fifteen years, a new batch of English majors would rediscover her stylish wit—but no new books had been written in nearly fifty years. Many were the speculations as to why Penelope Naughton had fled into obscurity—everything from an illegitimate pregnancy to incipient cirrhosis of the liver—and many were the reporters who tried to do a where-are-they-now number on her only to be sent away from her upstate ancestral home without even a glimpse of their quarry.

"She must be nearing ninety," Sigrid mused as she leafed through the folder.

Penelope Naughton's signature was a shaky scrawl on a notarized letter that gave Clayton Gladwell power of attorney to draw up a contract with Contempo Cinematics. The contract was dated two years earlier and now that she saw it, Sigrid seemed to remember having read something about a musical based on Penny Naughton's life being in the works. She thought she even recalled that they were looking for "a young Glenda Jackson who can sing" to play the lead.

"Clay was pleased at how much money he got Contempo to give her," said Nancy Kuipers, reading over Sigrid's shoulder. "Not that Miss Naughton especially needed it. Clay said she's still getting good royalties from her books. But she has several relatives to support, so it'll come in handy. He even made Contempo give her a percentage of the finished movie in addition to that advance; so if it hits big, cable and video will double her take."

Sigrid looked at the bottom lines. She didn't know what was usual in such cases, but the sum Clayton Gladwell had extracted from Contempo looked like good negotiating to her.

"You said there were originally over a dozen of these blue folders?" asked Sigrid. "These were the only remains we found. Where are the others?"

"These are all that are left," said Kuipers. "They were so special to Clay that when he decided to retire, he made appointments with everyone to turn the files back to them personally and to say goodbye. See?"

She turned the leaves in Gladwell's desk calendar and showed Sigrid the appointments the lawyer had scheduled. A Howard Tachs had seen him yesterday morning and Nichole Naughton was due that morning.

"She's Penelope Naughton's younger sister," said Mrs. Kuipers. Her pretty face was momentarily bemused. "Younger! She's at least eighty and her mind's starting to wander a bit, but she's still able to get around. Penelope is bedridden now."

"Who's Howard Tachs?" asked Sigrid.

"I'm not sure. I think he may own an art gallery here in midtown."

She pointed to Helmut Dussel's name, which appeared at the three o'clock slot for that afternoon, followed by the name William Burchlow in parentheses.

"He's the director of Mr. Dussel's nursing home,"

explained Kuipers. "He's bedridden, too, so Clay was going to turn his papers over to Mr. Burchlow."

The Bhattacherjeas were scheduled for Monday morning.

"And Mr. Trent?" asked Sigrid, flipping back to the previous day.

"Well, as you can see, he was here yesterday afternoon, but Clay must have planned to wait until after his grandson was back before closing out his file. Perhaps next week."

"There's no appointment for Elena Dorato," Sigrid noticed.

Nancy Kuipers looked at her oddly. "Elena Dorato's dead."

"I know," said Sigrid. "So who would he have given her folder to?"

CHAPTER V

■

By eleven, Tillie had finished his preliminary interviews with Gladwell's office staff and he and Sigrid were beginning to have a clear picture of the murdered attorney's last weeks of life as he wound down his practice.

Clayton Gladwell had made no secret of his determination to retire, and Sigrid was not surprised to hear that Millicent Barr had already lined up a new job in a nearby law firm, nor that Dan Embry was facing his own forced retirement without pleasure.

According to Tillie, Embry had feelers out at Columbia University for reference work and tutoring, but Jean Parrish was placidly living one day at a time and gave no sign of worrying whether or not the job market for secretaries was tight or wide open. She could type eighty words a minute with ninety-seven percent accuracy and seemed to feel that was insurance enough. Working for Clayton Gladwell the past eight years had been pleasant enough; working for someone else would be equally pleasant. A job was a job, wasn't it?

"Was there anything different about Mr. Gladwell yesterday?" Sigrid asked her.

The secretary considered, then shook her head slowly. "Just the same as ever."

Her plump hands wandered over the piles of paper

heaped on her desk. Her movements were slow and almost aimless, yet order was inexorably returning. Papers drifted back into their manila folders, folders into their proper file drawers.

Across the paper-strewn aisle separating her desk from the law library, Dan Embry huffed and bustled with busy energy, but Jean Parrish's lackadaisical efforts seemed to accomplish more.

Sigrid was intrigued. The woman barely glanced at each sheet, yet she was able to dispose of it almost automatically.

"You must remember every word you ever typed," Sigrid said.

"Not really. You get so you know what names go with which papers. Sort of the shape of the paragraphs, if you know what I mean."

Sigrid didn't, but Mrs. Parrish couldn't make it any clearer. "It just all fits together," she said blankly and continued doing it.

"Were you familiar with Mr. Gladwell's special blue files?" asked Sigrid.

"Sure."

"Do you remember Howard Tachs?"

The secretary hazarded a guess. "Was he one of the blue folders?"

"That's right," Sigrid said encouragingly. "He had a final appointment with Mr. Gladwell yesterday morning to pick up his papers and settle his account."

"I don't handle payment if Mrs. Kuipers is here."

"But you did type up letters or documents relating to Tachs's legal affairs, didn't you?"

"Was he the one who had so much trouble getting his fire insurance company to pay off?" wondered Mrs. Parrish.

"I don't know. Mrs. Kuipers thinks he owns an art gallery here in midtown."

"Oh, him."

"Well?" Sigrid asked patiently.

"Well, what?" Mrs. Parrish seemed bewildered.

Tillie thought it best to start all over again.

"Mrs. Parrish," he said gently, "we're trying to re-construct Mr. Gladwell's last day. Yesterday."

The woman nodded comfortably to show that she fol-lowed him.

"We know Mr. Gladwell got here about ten, dictated a letter to you first—"

"That's right," said Mrs. Parrish. "To a real estate agent about selling his apartment."

(Sigrid made a mental note to check out Gladwell's apartment. Not that she wanted to buy. And not that she could afford a wealthy lawyer's apartment. Still...)

"He conferred with Mrs. Kuipers a half hour or so," Tillie continued, "then Mr. Tachs arrived for his ap-pointment at eleven."

"I never meet clients unless Mr. Gladwell wants me to take notes," warned Mrs. Parrish.

"Mrs. Kuipers tells us that the blue-folder clients were special to Mr. Gladwell," said Sigrid. "Can you tell us what there was about Mr. Tachs that made him special?"

The secretary shrugged. "I wouldn't know about things like that."

"But if you were the one who typed up the contents of each folder—"

"I just did what Mr. Gladwell told me," said Jean Parrish. "I don't remember the details. There were con-tracts, bills of sale, stuff to do with paintings and sculp-tures, I suppose. How would I know what made something special to Mr. Gladwell? I'm just his secre-tary."

She stood up with the most firmness she'd shown here-tofore and announced that it was after eleven and she always had a second cup of coffee at eleven.

As she disappeared into the lounge across the hall, Dan Embry's rich chuckle reached Tillie and Sigrid.

"And there you have the eighth wonder of the world," he laughed. "A totally incurious woman."

He doffed an imaginary hat to Sigrid. "My apologies, Lieutenant, but surely you'll admit such complete lack of curiosity is unique among women?"

"Among men, too, I should think," Sigrid said coolly. "What about you, Mr. Embry?"

"Longest nose in the building," the cherubic old man admitted happily.

"So what do you know about Howard Tachs?" she asked.

"Nothing!" he beamed. "Isn't this an odd office? Those who are privy to state secrets couldn't care less; those who would care aren't in a position to know. I've worked here part-time for almost six years and I never even heard of blue folders till last week when Gladwell started calling clients in and returning them personally. Other current stuff's been going out by messenger or registered mail, but not the blue folders.

"Those went out clutched under the arms of clients who didn't look a bit sad when they left even though a couple looked like hell on wheels going in."

"Give me an example," Sigrid invited.

"Well, take Tachs. I could have told you he was blue-folder the minute he walked in. Sort of a hangdog look about him as if he thought he was going to get yelled at or horsewhipped. Twenty minutes in with Gladwell and out he comes, all smiles. Hands Mrs. Kuipers a nice fat envelope to settle his account, goodbyes all around, then he's dancing out of here like Fred Astaire on his way to meet Ginger Rogers."

"Maybe Mr. Gladwell had given him some good news about a lawsuit or something," suggested Tillie.

"Maybe," said Dan Embry, "But unless Tachs confides in you, you can't be sure, can you? Nancy Kuipers didn't know what was in his folder and Jean Parrish didn't care."

Anything he might have added was lost in a rise of querulous voices out by the reception desk.

"But, my dear young lady, we've an appointment," the elderly woman insisted.

Although she was quite old and finely wrinkled now, the remnants of great beauty still clung to the ivory face of Penelope Naughton's younger sister Nichole. Her rusty white hair was a thick tangle of close-cropped curls, her eyes were a clear green, and her nose was much less beaked than her more famous sister's. She carried her six-foot frame erectly and was using her tallness deliberately to intimidate the more diminutive Millicent Barr.

"I'll get Mrs. Kuipers!" cried the receptionist, who was unfazed by the woman's height but completely routed by Nichole Naughton's deafness.

"My appointment was with Mr. Gladwell," said the willful Miss Naughton to the girl's retreating back.

"She said he's dead, Aunt Nick," said the teenage boy at her elbow. He spoke in nearly normal tones and the old woman stared at him.

"*Dead?* Nonsense! We have an appointment."

Sigrid and Tillie followed Nancy Kuipers as she and Milly Barr joined the two newcomers.

The boy—slender and no more than seventeen, thought Sigrid—was as tall as his aunt, with the family nose and bright red hair. His face was also red with self-consciousness while he introduced himself as Peter Luft and the woman as his great-aunt, Nichole Naughton.

"I'm sorry you've come all this way for nothing," said Nancy Kuipers. "We called your home, but your mother said you'd already left."

"That's okay," said the boy, but his great-aunt refused to grasp the situation. "Three hours to get here and Mr. Gladwell won't see us? Disgraceful."

"Aunt Nick, he's been shot," the boy repeated patiently. "He's dead."

"Then who's in charge?"

"I am, Miss Naughton," said Nancy Kuipers loudly. "We've met before, remember? I was Mr. Gladwell's office manager."

The old woman opened her black straw purse and handed Kuipers a certified check. "Here," she said. "Now give me Penny's papers."

Mrs. Kuipers glanced at Sigrid, who shook her head.

Handing back the check, Kuipers said, "I'm so sorry, Miss Naughton, but the police can't let anything leave here until—"

"What's that?" Miss Naughton's green eyes flashed. "Can't?" she asked sharply.

Peter Luft tried to intervene, but she shook the boy's hand off abruptly.

"Ten thousand dollars," she told them. "That's what he said and that's what I brought."

Again she tried to give Kuipers the check. Her nephew reached out and pocketed it.

"Come away, Aunt Nick," he pleaded. "We're interrupting a police investigation. We'll get Aunt Penny's papers another time."

The old woman's militance collapsed. "Police?" she faltered, looking at Sigrid and Detective Tildon. "But we brought the money," she said plaintively.

"And we'll get it straightened out later," the boy promised. He slipped her arm through his and turned to Nancy Kuipers with as much dignity as he could muster. "When everything's so that we can settle Aunt Penny's account, would you please call us?"

"Certainly," said Mrs. Kuipers sympathetically. "Tell your aunts not to worry about a thing."

CHAPTER VI

▌

"A certified check?" murmured Tillie as he and his lieutenant watched Peter Luft guide Miss Naughton away through the wide double doors.

"And Embry said Tachs settled his account yesterday with a fat envelope," said Sigrid in a voice equally low. "Cash?"

They moved away from Milly Barr's desk and sharp little ears into the open conference room.

"Last night I noticed that one of those blue folders had an FBI report inside," said Tillie, "but I didn't have time to read anything. What's actually there?"

"Nothing special that I could see," said Sigrid and gave him a quick rundown on the five remaining folders. "Three of them were prominent people though: Elena Dorato was a world-famous actress; Penelope Naughton was a writer and a well-known symbol of café society in the thirties here in New York; and you know what Justin Trent represents. If his grandson has really been found, it'll be a seven-day wonder. Nevertheless, if we're talking extortion, it wasn't obvious from those files.

"You read over them though, Tillie. You're better at spotting a discrepancy than I am."

It was said matter-of-factly. In the time that they'd been working together, Sigrid had come to rely on Tillie's penchant for detail and preferred him, with his dogged, by-the-book thoroughness, to others in the department with flashier reputations for brilliance. Together, they were making a quiet reputation of their own for competence and a high percentage of cases solved.

"After the folders," said Tillie, "I wouldn't mind a quick browse through Gladwell's account books."

"Okay, but try not to get bogged down. And try not to let Nancy Kuipers know what you're looking for. She and Gladwell planned to marry next month and I don't think she'd like it if she thought we suspected her fiancé of blackmailing."

"Wouldn't she know if he was?"

"Not necessarily. She may be a consummate actress, but as cooperative and open as she's been so far, I can't believe she thinks Clayton Gladwell was anything less than wonderful," Sigrid said dryly. "She honestly seems to think the folders were just Gladwell's sentimental favorites and that he didn't confide in her because of the ethics involved."

"Embry must suspect something odd, though," said Tillie. "Remember his remark about those who might have put two and two together not being allowed to know while those who knew didn't care?"

"Meaning Jean Parrish," Sigrid agreed. "She certainly is a cow. I've seen parking meters that take more interest in their surroundings than she does."

Tillie grinned and Sigrid glanced at her watch. Almost noon.

"I think I'll try to catch Howard Tachs at his gallery," she said. "Want to break for lunch?"

But Tillie was too eager to get started on Gladwell's papers to leave, so Sigrid had a chicken salad sandwich sent up from the coffee shop on the first floor as she passed through the lobby.

Afterward, she walked along East Thirty-fourth Street, planning to take the Sixth Avenue subway uptown. The July sun smoldered above hazy skies and she could feel the sidewalk's heat beneath the soles of her shoes.

At Altman's, a dress in the window caught her eye simply because it was bare-shouldered and long and because the male mannequin was wearing white tie and tails. It reminded her that Nauman was expecting to see her in something more formal than workaday pantsuits, come tomorrow night.

Howard Tachs could wait another fifteen minutes, she decided, ducking into Altman's air-conditioned coolness.

There were very few things that Sigrid Harald enjoyed shopping for and clothes were nowhere on that short list. Altman's possessed a dazzling array of dresses, dresses appropriate for dancing everything from rock to Rachmaninoff—but on someone else, thought Sigrid, retreating from ruffles and sequins, the sleek little wisps of nothing and the dramatically designed "big statements."

In less than ten minutes she was back out on the sizzling pavement, berating herself for cowardice. If she could ask perfect strangers for alibis, motives for murder or intimate details about their lives with a victim, what was so hard about explaining her needs to a salesclerk?

She crossed Fifth Avenue, gritted her teeth and plunged into Dunlap's. This time she even went so far as to tell an unoccupied clerk, "I need something formal. Preferably long and cool and not too tight. For dancing."

The saleswoman took in Sigrid's tall, thin, and minimally curvaceous form, murmured something about the innocent look and soon returned with an armful of blue dotted swiss.

"Not *that* innocent," Sigrid protested.

The clerk's next choice resembled a pair of black organza bell-bottomed pajamas shot through with red metallic threads.

Sigrid looked at herself in the mirror.

"Of course," said the clerk, "you should be wearing very high, very red slingbacks and your hair should be loose or, better yet, teased into three times the fullness. And with red combs—"

"I think something a little more . . ."

"Traditional?" said the woman, undaunted. "Perhaps you're right. I know just the thing."

She buttoned Sigrid into a long oriental coatdress of pale pink satin with mandarin collar and short butterfly sleeves, heavily embroidered with birds and flowers. "Your hair pulled back in a chignon is perfect for this," she said enthusiastically. "Now if you have long earrings . . . maybe pink jade and pearls?"

"I don't," said Sigrid. Nor, she thought, catching a glimpse of the price tag, did she have eight hundred dollars to spend on one dress when she would soon be out on the streets homeless.

She disentangled herself from the clerk, put on her own clothes and finished trekking to Herald Square. On the steps of the subway, she paused and looked across at Macy's. That was probably where she should have looked in the first place instead of wasting time in Altman's and Dunlap's. There was probably nothing she'd really like there either, but at least Macy's was more in line with her pocketbook. She could be just as dissatisfied for half the cost.

Suddenly realizing the silliness of that line of logic, Sigrid switched her mind back to official matters as trains rumbled by beneath her feet.

CHAPTER VII

Howard Tachs's gallery was on the second floor of a building in the West Fifties. Since meeting Oscar Nauman, Sigrid had become familiar with the layout of these small galleries. From the street, one walked down a narrow hall to a tiny birdcage of an elevator built to hold about two and a half people and which took three minutes to rise from one floor to the next. This elevator, a confection of beveled mirrors and japanned wood, was slower than usual, but it debouched upon the usual picture-hung hallway with an equally predictable suspicious-eyed young man standing before the gallery office. Small black-and-purple woodcuts lined the walls.

"Howard Tachs?" asked Sigrid.

"Inside," the youth gestured.

Sigrid passed through the arched doorway at the end of the parqueted hall into a large bright room. The white walls were devoted to big pastel-colored portraits of houses that, for some reason, suggested Bedford Avenue in Brooklyn. *Lower* Bedford Avenue—early in the spring probably, but late in the afternoon. The wooden, deadpan obviousness of these pictures made Nauman label them the "Front Porch School," yet such works were popular and seemed to sell well. Xeroxed copies of a flattering review from that prestigious art magazine, *The*

Loaded Brush, were placed around the room at impossible-to-miss intervals.

Sigrid was neither angered nor amused by the vapid canvases. Unlike Nauman, who felt the need of a minimal level of intelligence or wit in any art, she was indifferent to most periods outside the late Gothic.

Howard Tachs possessed the face of a complacent middle-aged rodent. He had sandy hair running to gray, faded blue eyes, and his thin nose and mouth came together in a point somewhat reminiscent of a self-important field mouse.

As Sigrid approached, he gave her a warm smile but continued his attention to the other occupant of the room, a well-dressed matron who seemed torn between two pictures. One was the portrait of a white, two-story frame house with gingerbread trim and white wicker rocking chairs visible upon its blue-shadowed porch. The other could have been a rear view of the same house.

"Oh, dear," Sigrid heard the woman say. "Which do you think?"

"Now, Mrs. Delgano—"

"Oh, you're right!" she said impulsively. "It's mad but I shall take them both. They so want each other, don't you think?"

"Perceptive as always, Mrs. D.," said Tachs. "The synergistic impact of *two* Morgenbergs—" A moment of silence as they contemplated the impact—"No," Tachs said fervently, "you'll not regret it."

The woman allowed him to waft her toward the door only after he'd promised to send over the two pictures the *minute* the show closed next week.

"So sorry to make you wait," said Tachs when the woman was finally gone. "But how nice to see you again."

Sigrid looked blank.

"Weren't you at the opening of the Diller retrospective with Oscar Nauman last month?"

"Why, yes, but I don't think—"

"No, we didn't actually meet," Tachs smiled. "I handed you a glass of wine, but we weren't formally introduced. I'm afraid Oscar doesn't have a very high opinion of me or my artists. But then his mind's been closed for years, don't you find?"

"I hadn't noticed," Sigrid said.

The man's pale eyes sharpened and his nose seemed to twitch with interest. "No matter," he said. "Now how may I help you, Ms.—"

"Harald. Lieutenant Harald." She held out her ID folder and watched Howard Tachs's face become wary.

"How avant-garde of Oscar to have found *you*," he said gamely, but Sigrid would not be deflected.

"I'm here officially," she said. "I've just come from Clayton Gladwell's office."

Tachs drew back and his small pointed teeth were nearly bared beneath his short upper lip, but if Sigrid hoped to surprise him into a revealing remark, she was disappointed. He maintained his watchful tenseness.

"You were a client of his, I believe," she said.

"Is that what he told you?"

"It's what his staff told me. Mr. Gladwell is dead. Someone shot him late yesterday afternoon."

"Oh, dear!" The mouse face was poised for flight. "And?"

"And you were among the last to see him alive. Naturally we'd like to know what your meeting was about, what you discussed, your impression of his state of mind."

"What does his staff say we discussed?" asked Tachs.

"They're being discreet, of course," Sigrid said vaguely.

It didn't work. For the first time since Sigrid had identified herself, Tachs seemed to let out a deep breath. The friendly mouse smile was back on his lips again.

"I'm afraid I won't be able to give you much help, Lieutenant. My business with Mr. Gladwell was quite confidential. He was retiring, you see, and ending our association."

"He gave you back some special papers," said Sigrid.

"Personal papers, yes," Tachs agreed.

"We were wondering if they might have been incriminating documents for which Gladwell was blackmailing you."

Again the bared lips, but Tachs recovered more quickly this time. "Blackmail?"

"Did you really believe him when he said he wasn't keeping any copies of those papers?" Sigrid goaded, making an educated guess as to why Tachs had left Gladwell's office so light-footedly the day before.

"As a matter of fact, I did," he said boldly. "I still do. Why not? The heart condition was no secret. He had a retirement home picked out in southern France and a tax-free retirement fund that'd been building in a Swiss bank account. Whatever else he may have been, Clayton Gladwell wasn't mean-minded."

His nose twitched smugly. "Sorry, Lieutenant. If I tell you those were personal legal papers Gladwell returned yesterday, you've no way to disprove it, have you?"

Nor was he more helpful in describing his last meeting with Gladwell. The lawyer had been his usual imperturbable self—smooth, in control. No rubbing of salt in wounds, Sigrid gathered. If Gladwell had been a blackmailer, it sounded as if he conducted it much like legitimate business and that he'd wound up his association with Howard Tachs pleasantly, in a businesslike manner.

Tachs had tendered final payment to Gladwell's office manager and that was that.

"You weren't resentful enough to go back later with a gun?" asked Sigrid.

Tachs bared his teeth in a polite smile. "But don't take just my word for it," he said and gave her the name of a client who'd been in his gallery from four-thirty to five. Afterward, he and his assistant had spent the next hour and a half hanging those black-and-purple woodcuts in the hall. The artist and her lover had been there too, and then they'd all gone out for supper together.

Sigrid dutifully noted the names and addresses.

Howard Tachs accompanied her to the elevator, and as the narrow door closed between them he said throatily, "Love to Oscar, of course."

CHAPTER VIII

▌

By the time Sigrid grabbed a sandwich and returned to Gladwell's office, it was some few minutes before three and William Burchlow, the director of Helmet Dussel's nursing home over in Queens, had not yet arrived for his appointment.

Jean Parrish had made remarkable headway on her disrupted files and Milly Barr was doing her bit to sort and untangle, but Dan Embry had not returned from lunch.

Sigrid found Tillie still ensconced at Gladwell's desk, to the visible unhappiness of Nancy Kuipers. Her lover had been so discreet, so almost secretive with those blue files that it distressed her to see Tillie methodically poring over every sheet, to have strangers poke through papers she herself had never read.

Nor was she better pleased when Tillie turned from the folders to the office account books, which was what they were discussing when Sigrid returned.

A light flashed on the dead attorney's telephone, and while Nancy Kuipers reassured an anxious client that an estate settlement currently being steered through the court system would not necessarily be hindered by Gladwell's death, Sigrid gave Tillie a quiet description of her visit to Howard Tachs's gallery. Tillie was not surprised to hear their suspicions of blackmail tentatively confirmed; Tachs's mention of a Swiss account backed up his own conclusions.

"See?" he said, and pointed to the previous day's page in the account book. There were two checks entered, one by mail from a Texas investment firm for four hundred dollars, and Justin Trent's hundred thousand. Nothing else.

"I do see," said Sigrid.

"See what?" asked Mrs. Kuipers, replacing the receiver.

"Mr. Tachs said he settled his account here yesterday morning," said Sigrid, "but his payment doesn't seem to have been posted."

The fair-skinned office manager flushed a bright red. "I— We— It's in the safe," she stammered.

"Cash payments are handled separately?" Sigrid asked mildly.

The older woman dropped her eyes, but her features remained flushed. "Yes," she said. Then she looked at Sigrid defiantly. "What of it? You needn't act surprised. The way IRS gouges people like Clay, everybody in his bracket fudges a little on income taxes."

"Ten thousand isn't exactly fudging," Tillie objected.

"*Ten thousand?*" exclaimed Kuipers. "*Never!* There can't be more than five hundred in that envelope."

Before they could argue, she'd whirled from the room down the wide hall to her own office. She was back almost immediately with a long white envelope. "It's tens and twenties," she told them, "small bills Clay could just add to his wallet without anyone's noticing."

She took an ebony letter opener from Gladwell's desk and slit the envelope. "There!" she said and almost strangled on the word as twenty five-hundred-dollar bills spilled across the polished desktop.

"Add the certified check Miss Naughton tried to give you this morning and that's twenty thousand for two blue-folder clients," said Sigrid. "Were all of them contributing to his Swiss bank account?"

Nancy Kuipers was still staring at the money and

seemed bewildered. "Swiss account?" she asked. "Clay didn't—" She swallowed hard. "Did he?"

There was pain in her voice and Tillie answered gently, "We've been told so. Didn't you know?"

She shook her head slowly. "I never opened the envelopes, just put them in the safe for Clay and he took them home with him. I thought it was only a few hundred now and then. Ten thousand from Mr. Tachs! It's impossible—Clay only drew up a couple of routine documents for him . . . at least that's what he said."

Her eyes flicked to the stack of blue folders on the edge of the desk. "What could he have done for Howard Tachs to charge so much for so little time?" she asked them.

CHAPTER IX

A team from headquarters had just finished processing Gladwell's Gramercy Park apartment when Sigrid and Tillie arrived shortly after 3:30. The apartment, which Gladwell had so recently put on the market, occupied the entire third floor of a lovely townhouse built in the late 1800s.

"Well beyond *my* salary," Sigrid thought wryly as she stepped from the elevator.

The furnishings echoed those of Gladwell's law office: comfortably eclectic with a leaning toward French provincial. On the bookshelves in the study, porcelain figurines were interspersed with Book-of-the-Month Club selections still in their original glossy covers. Near an inviting reading chair, though, was a shelf of spy novels—John Le Carré, Eric Ambler, Somerset Maugham, even E. Phillips Oppenheim—which seemed to be well read. The phonograph albums beneath the stereo ranged from Broadway musicals to the light classics with an unexpected handful of German beer-hall bands mixed in.

And what, wondered Sigrid, did that tell them about Gladwell's character? Official bestsellers and spy stories, Offenbach and oompah bands. Was he a man of educated sensibilities with a taste for complex machinations or a simple peasant at heart?

46

She turned to the search team and heard them tell Tillie how they'd found little of interest in the apartment until they came here to the study.

"Look at the desk," they said.

The butternut kneehole desk was over a hundred years old, but it had been altered by a modern craftsman. When the bottom drawer was taken out and laid side by side with the two upper drawers, the difference in their length was obvious; but a less careful examination would have passed right over it. With the help of a flashlight they had found the simple spring catch, and now the contents of the desk's secret niche lay on the blotter beside a framed snapshot of Nancy Kuipers and a freckle-faced little girl. "We counted the money," said one of the officers. "Forty-six thousand."

They were commended for their thoroughness and dismissed for the day, then Sigrid reached across the neat stack of bills and picked up one of the two small green leather notebooks. It appeared to be a ledger of moneys sent to the bank in Berne, Switzerland. The neat list of figures began with a seventy-thousand-dollar deposit several years earlier, and the current total was over three quarters of a million.

Tillie opened the second notebook and smiled at Sigrid. "Here it is, Lieutenant: dates, figures, everything!"

"Names?"

"Just initials," he admitted. "That's almost as good."

It was a ledger of Clayton Gladwell's off-the-record transactions; the first date preceded the Swiss account by several months.

Tillie sat down at the desk, took a sheet of paper and began listing initials and dates as Sigrid read them aloud.

For the first year or so there was only one pair of initials. That was later joined by another; by the last entry they had transcribed several sets. Some of these had been discontinued through the years, and a small cross drawn after each last payment made Sigrid and Tillie decide those people had probably died.

Of the remaining eight, six matched Tillie's list of blue-folder names—Helmut Dussel, Elena Dorato, Morarji

Bhattacherjea, Penelope Naughton, Justin Trent and Howard Tachs.

"Well, we know E.D. can't stand for Elena Dorato," said Tillie. "She's dead."

"Probably someone else," Sigrid agreed. "There's only one cash payment for five thousand, a good ten years after Dorato drowned. Look here though." She pointed to the page entry. "*Further payment in kind.* Wonder what that means?"

"Maybe E.D. was involved in drugs or something like that and Gladwell was taking a cut of the goods," Tillie suggested.

"Perhaps," Sigrid said slowly.

"Wonder what he could have had on Penelope Naughton? Everything I've ever read about her sounds as if she'd laugh at the idea of scandal."

Sigrid shrugged. "No one ever learned why she left the city so abruptly and went into seclusion."

They went through the ledger again, noting the regular payments of one to five hundred dollars a month for all the initials except E.D. and J.T.

"If J.T. stands for Justin Trent," she mused, "it doesn't follow Gladwell's usual blackmail pattern. There's just one listing for seventy-five thousand, thirteen months ago."

"Maybe Gladwell jotted it down here simply because it was a cash payment he wasn't planning to report to IRS."

They agreed that H.D. was undoubtedly Helmut Dussel, for the first entry came shortly after the date Gladwell had located him in that Queens nursing home six years ago. Similarly, P.N. followed the contract he'd arranged between Penelope Naughton and Contempo Cinematics.

If H.T. was indeed Howard Tachs, the gallery owner had been paying Gladwell three hundred dollars a month for over two years. M.B. was the newest contributor to Gladwell's retirement fund: two installments of three hundred each.

"Millicent Barr or Morarji Bhattacherjea?" wondered Sigrid.

"Mrs. Kuipers said Dr. Bhattacherjea did the radiology work on Gladwell this spring," Tillie said. "March or April, so June's about right for his first payment."

They decided that the unidentified sets of initials probably represented the blue-folder clients Dan Embry had described to them that morning, because those carried recent dates and listed final payments of ten thousand each.

They almost missed the page marked *Dispersals* because it was only one sheet near the end of the book. There was but a single listing in Gladwell's precise writing: *$25,000 to D.S.—1st pmt.* The entry was dated April 12 of that year, about three months ago, and was followed by a small cross and a question mark.

"D.S.?" asked Tillie. He looked through the list of names this case had turned up so far and found no match.

"First payment to someone who has since died," said Sigrid. "Or at least Gladwell wondered if he'd died?"

They went through the rest of the papers on Gladwell's desk, and when nothing else pertinent turned up, they recounted the money, then Tillie sealed it and the ledgers inside sturdy manila evidence envelopes and they both initialed across the seals.

"I think perhaps I'll have a talk with Justin Trent," said Sigrid, "while you see what you can learn from the Bhattacherjeas."

CHAPTER X

I

In the director's office of the Lantana Walk Nursing Home, Helen Burchlow watched her husband punch the buttons on his telephone handset and said, "I still think you ought to go down there."

"I know what I'm doing, Helen," he said calmly. "Kindly be silent for a moment."

He waited until he heard Clayton Gladwell's receptionist answer, then said smoothly, "This is William Burchlow. I was to have met this afternoon with Mr. Gladwell on behalf of Mr. Dussel and I just learned of his unfortunate death last night. May I ask if anyone will be taking on Mr. Gladwell's practice?"

He frowned as Millicent Barr went through the non-committal formula she'd been repeating all day. "I see. Very well, Miss Barr, I shall tell Mr. Dussel he can expect to hear from your office in the next week or so. Thank you."

"Well?" asked Helen Burchlow. She was a mild, sandy-haired matron of middle years, almost a female clone of her husband, who was also sandy-haired and slightly plump. His tailored twill carried a well-known label; her simple shirt dress was a natural cotton creation from Saks. There was nothing flashy in his gold cuff links and antique gold wristwatch, nor in her pearls and the neat circle of diamonds that constituted her wedding band.

"Whatever Gladwell guessed," he reminded her again, "there was nothing he could prove. Don't forget that, my love."

"But the police must be there," she said, nervously twisting her strand of pearls. "They'll be going through his papers. They'll find out."

"Gladwell had a large practice, Helen. They won't go through every scrap of paper and even if they do, I doubt if Gladwell kept records of our transactions. Now do stop pulling on your necklace before you break it again. If we just sit tight and—"

The intercom on his desk buzzed and he pressed a switch. "Yes, Rosa?" he said in his pleasant, well-modulated voice.

"You wanted to know if anyone asked for Mr. Dussel," said his receptionist from the front desk.

"Someone here for Dussel? Who?"

"I'm not sure, Mr. Burchlow. That new orderly—Higgins—just reported that a fat little man was up in Mr. Dussel's room when he passed by a few minutes ago. Whoever he is, he didn't register with *me!*"

"Thank you, Rosa," he said grimly and strode from his office toward the nearest staircase, leaving his wife to finger her pearls anxiously.

By the time William Burchlow reached the second floor, Dan Embry was already half a block away. This trip across the East River had been a total waste of time, he scolded himself. It hadn't occurred to him that Helmut Dussel might have lost what little English he ever knew and that, in his old age, he would have reverted so completely to the German speech of his childhood. Except for please and thank you, the only German Gladwell's pudgy little law clerk knew was goodbye.

Ruefully, he'd smiled at the bedridden old man and said, *"Auf Wiedersehen, Herr Dussel."*

There were another couple of strings to his bow, though, he remembered. He retraced his steps to the subway stop and a bank of telephones with directories for all five boroughs. Flipping through the Bronx white pages, he found a number which he carefully wrote down beside the name he'd seen earlier that day among the papers he'd helped Jean Parrish sort. Gladwell had been careful about not letting his left hand see how his right hand was stacking the deck, but he hadn't been able to keep Daniel Cicero Embry from picking up a few of the cards that had fallen on the floor.

Chuckling at his own cleverness, Embry inserted his coins in the pay phone, dialed, and when someone at the other end answered, he said, "This is Detective Tildon of the NYPD. We're investigating a homicide and I wonder if you can give us some information?"

Howard Tachs was seated in his office at the gallery, very much aware of his young assistant who sat at the next desk correcting proofs of their catalog for a major Piers Leyden exhibit scheduled for September.

The older man's eyes drifted to the painting over his desk that concealed a safe whose combination he alone knew despite Claude's sulkiness over that point.

He'd told Claude that he had destroyed the folder he'd brought back from Clayton Gladwell's office yesterday morning.

Now was the time to learn once and for all if Claude stayed from affection or because Tachs's monthly payments had kept Gladwell from sending the evidence to the police.

"I'll never forget this," Claude had blubbered gratefully two years ago. Back then he'd been scared silly of what could happen to his soft young body in a prison population, but he'd gotten smart-mouthed and resentful lately, and today he'd been an arrogant s.o.b.

A passing restlessness or a prelude to splitting?

Counting yesterday's buyback, Tachs figured he had around eighteen thousand invested in keeping Claude out of prison, and he didn't intend to see it go down the drain. He hadn't yet decided what he'd do if Claude tried to leave, but if Lieutenant Harald could have seen the expression on his face at that moment, she would have abandoned her impression of a friendly field mouse in favor of a malevolent cat.

At the sound of the slammed taxi door out by the front porch, the listening woman flew down the shadowed hall and fumbled with the door latch. "Peter?" she called.

"It's us, Mom," the red-haired boy replied. He handed their fare through the window of the dusty green-and-black checkered cab which served the small village. "Wait a minute, Aunt Nick, and I'll help you up the steps."

The old woman shook off his hand indignantly and marched up the whitewashed steps of her ancestral home without faltering. Afternoon sunlight glanced from her pinkish-white hair to gleam copper-bright on the auburn curls of the slender woman who stood waiting for them with the screen door open.

"Did you hear, Ellen? All that way for nothing. Nothing!"

"They called right after you left, Aunt Nick," said Ellen Luft. She felt her son's touch and turned to him anxiously. "What happened, Peter? What did they say?"

"Nothing, Mom. Don't worry. They'll be looking for that bastard's murderer down in the city. Nobody's going to come snooping around here. You'll see. It'll be all right."

But Peter Luft was only seventeen and it was hard for him to keep the tremor out of his voice.

In Bensonhurst, the air was hot and hazy. A warm and languid breeze barely ruffled the waves of lower New York Bay and did little to cool the land.

Nellie Goldenweiser lived in the bottom half of a brick-and-clapboard house set on a corner lot a block or so from Shore Parkway. The yard behind held a handsome pear tree and afforded a clear view of the Verrazano Bridge.

In her spotless kitchen, Nellie sliced a lime into a tall glass of ice and filled it with effervescent tonic water. Long ago she'd discovered that a gin and tonic tasted just as good without the gin.

Well, almost as good. It didn't fire the blood, of course; but it didn't leave you passed out and hung over either. It also didn't leave you with half-forgotten memories the next morning of passion and violence. A little wine at a seder or someone's bar mitzvah, that's all she should drink these days.

"Forget the gin, already," she told herself, "you're still a good age and strong enough to enjoy the rest of your life in peace now that Clayton Gladwell is dead."

She carried the cold wet glass outside to the lounge chair under her pear tree, eased her large feet out of the rundown carpet slippers she always wore at home, and stretched out with a comfortable sigh.

She liked to lie here on summer afternoons and watch the Verrazano go from gray to gold to gray again just before daylight vanished and the bridge lights came on to outline its graceful structure with twinkling firefly beauty.

"Tomorrow you should call New York," she remembered. "Tell them you don't need the money anymore."

An almost alcoholic glow of pleasure enveloped her as she thought of how Gladwell used to sit at his fancy desk while she oiled the wooden furniture in his office; how he would quote Robert Frost to her in his superior tone, little knowing how well she'd provided for herself.

Maybe just a tiny splash of gin to toast that sadistic schmuck's passage to hell? The liquor store was only five blocks away, but the thought of getting up, squeezing into a pair of street shoes and walking five blocks in this heat decided her. Instead, she lay back in the lounge chair, sipped her bitter tonic water, and watched airplanes from Kennedy and Newark crisscross the skies high above the bridge.

An hour's flying time to the west, the small blond boy looked out the plane window and sighed with boredom. Nothing to see except a floor of blue and white clouds.

At first it had been exciting sitting still while Aunt Rachel buckled him into the window seat, then straining against the belt to put his nose to the glass so he could watch the ground fall away and the buildings shrink to toy size. And it had been interesting to break through the clouds and see them up close. From the ground, clouds looked soft to him; up here, he thought they looked weird and rock-solid, and ultimately they bored him. On the movie screen several seats ahead, a man and woman talked and talked and if he knelt too long trying to see over the seats, his knees went to sleep and tingled unpleasantly. He sighed.

"Stop fidgeting!" said the woman beside him. She handed him the earphones and told him to tune into the kiddie channel again. "Listen to a story or some songs if you don't want to watch the movie," she said. "Just stop wiggling."

I'm too old to be a nursemaid, she thought. Thank the good Lord that detective found us so quick after Evvie died, before I wasted my hard-earned money buying him new clothes or tried to get him registered for first grade, and him without any birth certificate or shot record.

And hadn't it been just like Evvie to dump all her responsibilities? Steal somebody's kid and then park it on her. She'd known all along there was good and proper reason why she didn't take to the brat. The Bible said to feed and clothe the homeless orphan and she was prepared to do her duty, but when that phone call came telling her Evvie's boy was somebody else's, she wasn't one bit surprised. Hadn't she known it in her bones that that skinny little creature wasn't blood kin?

The boy's head sagged against her arm and she looked down to see that he'd fallen asleep. Even though he was going to wrinkle her new blouse, she let him be.

I've been good to him these past two months since Evvie died, she thought, and I can go on being good another day or two.

That detective said his grandfather was rich. A rich man could be right grateful that somebody'd been so good to his grandson.

CHAPTER XI

The front bell of the East Side townhouse chimed discreetly. Except for the new nursemaid, all servants had been given the afternoon and evening off, so it was Justin Trent himself who crossed the polished marble foyer to answer the door.

His daughter appeared on the landing above, her fragile body tense with expectation. "Is she here already?"

"Now, Sarah, it's much too soon," said Trent, blending reproach with indulgence. "Please, dear, you mustn't expect too much."

"I'm not, Father. It's just that . . ." Her voice trailed off, but her face glowed as she turned from the landing and Trent was encouraged to see that her shoulders no longer slumped with that old air of defeat and resignation. If this worked out, Sarah could be well again, beautiful and vibrant, with everything to live for. If not . . .

The bell chimed again and he pushed away the dark memory of his only child's slashed wrists last year when she had given up.

He opened the door to a vaguely familiar young woman. Trent prided himself on his politician's memory for names, but he had to grope for this one. "Sergeant— Childe, is it?"

"Harald," she said in a clear neutral voice. "And it's Lieutenant now, Mr. Trent."

She was too thin, he thought, and the tan pantsuit she wore did nothing to flatter. Her hair was braided into a plain knot and her face was bare of makeup.

Trent, who'd always been surrounded by stunning women, wondered why he remembered this plain-faced policewoman at all. She had been a nonentity four years ago, outranked and outclassed by all the high-powered local and federal professionals who'd been brought in as befitted a kidnapping that involved a man of Justin Trent's wealth and power.

"May I come in, Mr. Trent?"

"Yes of course, Lieutenant."

He held the door wider and a blast of hot muggy air flowed into the air-conditioned coolness.

"I'll be as brief as possible," she said as Trent directed her into his study. "We're questioning everyone Clayton Gladwell had seen recently."

"A terrible thing," Trent said automatically and gestured to a chair. He seated himself behind a carved walnut desk. "If there's any way I can help—"

"You were among the last to see him yesterday afternoon. Did he seem worried or apprehensive?"

"Clay Gladwell?" Trent smiled at the suggestion of that smooth and polished attorney showing fear. "I'm sure being murdered a few hours later was the farthest thing from his mind, Lieutenant. In any event, my visit with him was brief as his staff has no doubt told you."

"You gave him a check for one hundred thousand dollars," she said. "It seems rather a lot even for a lawyer like Mr. Gladwell."

"Part of it was a bonus," Trent said stiffly.

"For success?"

"I don't reward failure."

"Gladwell seems to have been very successful," she agreed. "Of course, we're beginning to think he wasn't exactly handicapped by morals."

Her phrasing appeared to amuse him. "You don't believe the ends ever justify the means?"

She didn't answer, but her wide gray eyes were cool and unwavering as she considered him, not his question. Trent suddenly remembered that steady consideration from four years ago, and for the first time he felt a small flick of apprehension. This young policewoman might be graceless and unattractive, but there was intelligence in those eyes. He was relieved when she dropped them to remove some papers from her briefcase.

"We've learned that Gladwell was closing out all his cases."

"Yes, a bad heart was making him retire early."

"In luxury, it would seem," said Sigrid. "Your hundred thousand would certainly help there. Not to mention the earlier payment—*cash* payment—you gave him."

"The money was for services rendered and I wasn't his only client."

"You seem to be the wealthiest."

Justin Trent's chin came up at that. "Do you suggest I paid Gladwell off for something and then murdered him?"

"Not at all, Mr. Trent. I merely suggest that information worth a hundred thousand to you might be equally attractive to someone else trying to silence Gladwell before he could pass it on to you or to us."

"I rather doubt that." Trent rose, a vigorous, well-built man who looked younger than the late fifties Sigrid knew him to be. "My business with Clay Gladwell had nothing to do with his murder. And now if you'll excuse me, Lieutenant, I must ask you to leave. I have another appointment soon."

"Rachel Elsner? I thought her plane wasn't due in until after six."

That stopped him in mid-stride and he slowly sat down again. "What do you know about Rachel Elsner?"

"Not very much," she said. "Only what Gladwell's office manager knew. He seems to have had a double filing system and your file was one of several which he kept so confidential that even she doesn't know all the details. In fact, she doesn't know what, if anything, is missing. It's possible that Gladwell's killer was trying to get back something incriminating, or perhaps he planned to try some blackmail on his own. Your file seems to carry such potential. There's no statute of limitations on kidnapping and it's one crime that still carries stiff penalties. How Rachel Elsner relates to your grandson may even make her a target for danger. That's why we're asking your help."

Late afternoon sunlight streamed through the rear windows of the study and haloed Trent's steel-gray hair as he considered. At last he compromised. "Tell me how much you've guessed and I'll tell you if you're correct."

"Very well." She consulted the notes she and Tillie had compiled in the last twenty-four hours. "We've learned that you first hired Gladwell about three years ago, less than a year after your grandson Jamie Logan disappeared. Is that correct?"

"The official investigation had dragged into nothing, the private detectives were useless and my daughter was distraught." Justin Trent's voice was steady but remembered pain lay behind his words. "I had to do something to give her hope."

Jamie Logan's disappearance had made all the national wire services, and the front page of every major newspaper had carried a photograph of the missing two-year-old. There were photos of his mother, a luminous Sarah Trent Logan, both as she'd looked at a glittering embassy ball somewhat earlier and as she made her pleas on television, tear-swollen, unraveled, and already teetering on the edge of her first nervous breakdown. And there were photos of his handsome young father, a twice-wounded Medal of Honor hero who'd survived Vietnam only to die in a civilian plane crash six months before the kidnapping.

Finally there were photos of Justin Trent, a millionaire several times over, reduced to common humanity by the loss of his grandson, a man who'd prided himself on infallibility and who now carried full blame.

By repetition, the story was soon familiar in its smallest details. Jamie Logan had been a bright, good-natured tot, surrounded from birth by smiling faces, his every need lavishly supplied, the heir to two fortunes and the golden apple of Justin Trent's eye. The financier had adored his young grandson and had taken every opportunity to sneak the child away from his nurse, an old-fashioned English nanny with strict ideas about sweets, balanced meals, and nap times.

On that hot summer day four years ago, Nanny had settled Jamie for a nap and had gone down to the kitchen when Justin Trent came along the hall, heading for the marina to try out the new speedboat he'd just bought as a toy for himself and Jamie.

In a statement that struck a chord of sympathy with every man who'd ever been separated from his grandson by female officiousness, Trent had confessed, "Jamie was supposed to be napping, but hell! He was just lying there, wide awake and singing to himself. I knew Nanny wouldn't miss him for an hour or so and I didn't think it would hurt him to skip his nap for once."

Television cameras followed Justin Trent's description of that last sunlit afternoon together, how they'd slipped out of the house unnoticed and driven across the George Washington Bridge to a busy marina on the New Jersey side of the Hudson.

The cameras lingered on the shiny new speedboat bobbing at its mooring, then panned over a sleek white Cadillac while the newscaster's voice repeated Trent's words: "We'd played hooky longer than I'd expected and Jamie was getting hungry and sleepy. I bought him a chocolate bar, settled him in the back seat of the car and walked over to the marina restaurant to call home. I didn't want Nanny to worry when she found his bed empty. When I got back to the parking lot, Jamie was gone."

The cameras zoomed in on the white leather interior of the car to focus poignantly on the crumpled chocolate wrapper, the last trace of little Jamie Logan.

Within the hour police were swarming over the entire area, but no Jamie. Along the waterside on such a hot summer day women with toddlers and baby carriages were not uncommon, but no one had seen Jamie taken. Without witnesses there was nothing to do except wait for the ransom note; when no ransom note appeared, fear lengthened into despair.

An FBI agent accompanied by an uncomfortable police commissioner broke the news as gently as possible to Sarah Logan and her father.

"We've examined all possibilities, Mrs. Logan. No ransom note probably means that whoever took your son wanted a child, not money. We've checked every known child molester and we've investigated every mother in a fifty-mile radius who's had a baby die in the last two years. Nothing. I'm sorry, but unless our inquiries turn up someone with an unexplained child, there's no other way to trace him."

"And that's it?" cried Sarah Logan. "You're quitting? You can't!" She clutched Trent's arm. "They can't, Father! Don't let them stop!"

In shrill and desperate sobs she begged for her son's recovery until a nurse came and helped her back to her room.

The FBI agent had sighed and told Trent, "In cases like this where we've eventually found the child, it was often healthy and unhurt. They aren't all taken by sexual perverts. Sometimes it's just someone who wants to be a parent."

"That's right," the commissioner chimed in. "It probably won't comfort her, but maybe you could help Mrs. Logan realize there's a good possibility that whoever took the boy will love him and look after him well."

"You're quite right," Trent had answered bleakly. "Such rationalization won't comfort my daughter."

"That's when I hired private investigators," Trent told the listening policewoman. "And after they got nowhere, I turned to Clayton Gladwell. He had a reputation for getting results."

"And now, after all this time, you think he'd found your grandson?"

"Is that what his secretary told you?"

She looked down at her notes again. "Gladwell seems to have spent the first few months going over the same ground we did. But he evidently thought this was worth noting."

She slid a Xeroxed sheet across the polished surface of his desk. The article carried a three-year-old California dateline and concerned drug culture and commune life. Someone had drawn a red ring around two paragraphs in particular:

> During the protest movement of the late sixties and early seventies, many young mothers deliberately failed to register the birth of male infants. "If the hawks don't know I have a son, they can't send him a draft notice 18 years from now," said one.
>
> It is estimated that several hundred male infants were never issued birth certificates. Since then the number may have grown to thousands, and includes both sexes as counterculture parents elect to dispense with what they term the "hassles of bureaucratic red tape." Unregistered midwives and the rise of home births have made this avoidance simple.

Trent glanced over the sheet and slid it back to her. "I remember when Gladwell brought this clipping to my attention. He said this might explain how my grandson was escaping notice. The FBI checked all the little boys in this area for which there were birth certificates, but there must have been several unregistered births that slipped by them."

Sigrid remembered the thorough search. She'd been one of those who'd pulled death certificates and called on bereaved parents to check that the missing two-year-old wasn't filling someone else's empty crib.

For the past few minutes she had been wishing she had traded places with Tillie. As a man, as a father, he might have established a better rapport with Justin Trent. Just as she was ready to call it quits for the day, Trent heaved a great sigh and gave a palms-up gesture of capitulation.

"There's no point in trying to hide things from you," he said. "I know you're only doing your job, Lieutenant, so I'll have to rely on your discretion. Just try to remember that if we have the media swarming all over us too soon, it could upset everything."

He searched her thin face carefully, probed the depths of those clear gray eyes, then nodded as if he felt he could trust what he saw there.

"You're quite correct that Gladwell has found my grandson," he said. "At least, we think he has. Jamie was only two when he vanished, you know. Still a baby. But this boy looks like him. He's the right age, the right coloring, the right blood type and he was being passed off as the son of a woman whose own child died here in New York a few days before Jamie disappeared.

"The young woman herself died of a drug overdose in California just a few weeks before Gladwell's detective found her, but her sister—Rachel Elsner—was next of kin and took him in. Gladwell says—" he broke off and looked embarrassed. "Sorry, it's hard to remember him in the past tense.

"Gladwell *said* that Rachel Elsner is a religious fundamentalist who considered her sister Evelyn to be a lost soul steeped in sin and perdition.

"Poor Jamie's had a rough four years—bouncing around the country, the woman he thought of as his mother spaced out on drugs most of the time, and now placed with an aunt who sounds like something out of Dickens."

Trent shook his head bitterly. "I've already been in touch with Dr. Jesov. He's the best child psychiatrist in New York. He's agreed to take Jamie on, help him understand what's been happening, try to keep his emotions on an even keel till he can come to terms with all this."

"Then you're totally convinced he *is* your grandson?" asked Sigrid.

"I am," Trent said simply.

"And Mrs. Logan?"

"She isn't sure. So far, all she's seen is a Polaroid snapshot of the boy. My daughter—" There was pain in the proud man's eyes as he appealed to Sigrid Harald for understanding. "She's had her hopes crushed so many times, Lieutenant, that she's almost afraid to let herself believe it's him. As soon as he's really here, as soon as she can touch him, put her arms around him, I'm sure she'll realize it *is* Jamie. That's why I want to keep the press away, keep it all low-key until Sarah's had a chance to meet him quietly. In the meantime, I'm just trying to go on with my life as usual and not let myself think of what it will mean to us to have Jamie back."

Sigrid was moved by the humanizing anguish and anticipation in the financier's bearing, and she appreciated that he could have ensured her cooperation by a short phone call to any of her superiors in the department. Yet there had been no hint of the pressure he could bring to bear, only an appeal to her fairness.

"We've no need to question Rachel Elsner immediately," she said, "however—"

"Yes?"

"It's only routine, Mr. Trent, something we've asked everyone connected with this case so far."

"You want my alibi?" asked Trent, mildly incredulous.

Sigrid started to explain again, but Trent held up forestalling hands.

"Never mind, Lieutenant. I understand the need for regulations and routine. When did it actually happen?"

"Somewhere around five-thirty is the current estimate."

"Let me think . . . my appointment with Gladwell was for three-thirty, and it must have been nearly four when we finished. I'd dismissed my chauffeur earlier, so I walked the few blocks up to the Pierpont Morgan Library. I was too keyed up over the news that Jamie was actually coming today to go back to my office, and anyhow there was a new exhibition of drawings I hadn't seen yet."

"The Mabuses?" murmured Sigrid.

"Why, yes," he said, surprised somehow that a police officer would be conversant on an obscure sixteenth-century artist.

He waited for an elucidation; when none came he continued, "I must have left around five—perhaps one of the guards will remember—and I decided to cut across to the Public Library and see if they had a decent biography of Mabuse. There was such a crush of people at the call desk, though, that I decided it could wait.

"By then it was rush hour, traffic was snarled, impossible to get a cab. It seemed just as fast to walk and I needed the exercise, so that's what I did. It must have been around six when I got home. One of the servants would be able to tell you if you wish to speak to them tomorrow."

"Did you see anyone you knew while walking home?"

Trent shook his head regretfully. "I'm sorry, Lieutenant. Not much of an alibi, is it? I suppose I might just have been able to rush back from the library, kill Gladwell, and then jog twenty-five blocks back between five-thirty and six o'clock."

"Do you jog?" Sigrid asked gravely.

"No," the man smiled.

"Do you own a gun?" she asked in the same tone.

In answer, he unlocked a desk drawer and drew out a Smith & Wesson .22 revolver. Sigrid lifted it to her nose and smelled only a metallic oiliness. It didn't seem to have been fired since its last cleaning and was fully loaded. She compared the serial number with the permit Trent had produced and asked, "May I borrow this for a few days?"

"Gladwell was killed with a .22?"

"We don't have the ballistics report yet," Sigrid said.

"Then you *do* think I could have killed him?" said the man, looking at her quizzically.

"Not at all, Mr. Trent. As you said, regulations and routine."

She gave him a receipt, tucked the gun into her briefcase and stood up. "You do understand, though, that we have to speak to Miss Elsner as soon as it's feasible?"

"Of course, Lieutenant."

They crossed the foyer to the front door and Trent drew her attention to a small drawing by Hans Burgkmair, a contemporary of Mabuse.

"Very nice," said Sigrid. "It reminds me of a Lucas Cranach at the Metropolitan."

"Similar styles," the financier agreed. He opened the door for her to leave and impulsively extended his hand.

Her hand was cool in his, but the firmness with which she returned his shake reminded him of his earlier uneasiness.

There was no way of knowing how much Clayton Gladwell had kept in his head and how much he'd put on paper, but Trent knew he could not afford to underestimate Lieutenant Harald's intelligence.

CHAPTER XII

▌

The Bhattacherjeas' address was an ornate brick apartment building lavishly decorated with molded terra-cotta both inside and out. It had been built around 1890, and since it stood in the middle of the Brooklyn Heights historic district, Tillie knew its large apartments would be matched by equally large rents.

Inside, the building was well kept; but even though the temperature here was a few degrees lower than outside, the arched and columned lobby seemed airless. There was no attendant on duty so Tillie had to scout past numerous cul-de-sacs for the self-service elevator.

It rose ponderously to the fifth floor and to a long narrow hallway made even darker by heavy maroon carpeting. Around the corner from the elevator he found the number he sought, but had to push the doorbell three times before the heavy door opened on a brass chain and a little girl peered through the crack.

No more than ten or eleven years old, she had dark skin, short, tight pigtails, and timid eyes the color of bitter chocolate. Her features were more negroid than East Indian. She was barefoot this hot July day and her yellow print sundress was a little too big. It dipped below her knees to give her an old-fashioned quaintness. Behind her, Tillie could see three smaller boys, all in short pants, crowding around for a peep through the narrow opening.

"Is Dr. Bhattacherjea at home?" he asked.

The little girl shook her head mutely.

"When do you expect them back?"

More silence, then the tallest of the other three, a bright-eyed little boy, spoke to her in words Tillie couldn't understand. Tillie decided that she must be Mrs. Bhattacherjea's East African niece and probably hadn't learned English fluently yet. He asked again, slower; but she shook her head and began to close the door.

Around the corner, the elevator chimed and the child hesitated at the rumble of those doors opening. As a short, dark-haired woman in a white lab coat rounded the corner, the girl undid the chain and held the door wide. The woman frowned at the sight of Tillie and her eyebrows questioned his presence.

"Dr. Bhattacherjea?" he asked.

She nodded, gave the bag of groceries she carried to the girl and paused on the threshold of her apartment.

Tillie gave his name and showed her his identification. "We're questioning everyone connected with Clayton Gladwell. You've heard of his death?"

"Yes. My husband is making his X rays." Her small bones carried several extra pounds, and the buttons of her lab coat strained across the lavender-and-purple cotton dress underneath. Perspiration gleamed on her upper lip along the line of a faint moustache and her eyes became more guarded.

"Will your husband be home soon?"

"No, he is staying late duty tonight," she said. Over her shoulder, she spoke sharply to the children and all four scurried from the vestibule.

Her uneasiness was almost palpable. Probably afraid they knew what Gladwell was blackmailing her husband for, Tillie thought. To relieve the tension, he asked pleasantly, "Was that the child whose papers Mr. Gladwell helped with?"

"Now, please, you go," said Mrs. Bhattacherjea. She stepped inside the vestibule and began closing the door.

"My husband—Tomorrow my husband is speaking to you."

The door closed firmly.

"She's definitely nervous about something and it may be connected with the little girl," Tillie said from the telephone booth in the lobby, "but she's not going to talk without her husband. I'll drop by tomorrow."

"Tomorrow's Saturday," Lieutenant Harald reminded him from her desk at headquarters.

"Yeah, well, I've been promising the kids we'd walk across the Brooklyn Bridge ever since its hundredth birthday celebration. If the weather's nice, I can combine business with pleasure. Otherwise I'll send Lowry. I've already got him checking the alibis of Gladwell's office staff, so he's familiar with the details. I'll let you know if I learn anything."

Sigrid hung up and her gray eyes became unfocused with a faraway look as she thought about walking across the Brooklyn Bridge.

With children. Children of her own.

With the towers of lower Manhattan gleaming to the left, river traffic below, helicopters and gulls wheeling in the blue sunshine; with the smell of the city that was uniquely its own, compounded from bus fumes, salt air, and a hundred different ethnic cuisines; and with children to grasp one's hand and cry, "Look at this!" or "What's that?"

She believed herself immune to baby fever, that inexplicable sudden hungering for a child of one's own womb that often overtook career women who had decided against bearing children. She liked her work, was good at it, and moreover had never met a man whose genes she wanted to combine with hers in perpetuity. (Oscar Nauman's face bobbled to the surface of her daydreaming mind and was promptly pushed back under.) Yet, her biological clock continued to tick away the years and she wondered how she'd feel when the choice was no longer hers. Regret? Resignation? Or simple relief?

Two weeks back, after being caught with all her excuses down, she'd spent the weekend at her cousin Hilda's out in Port Jefferson. Now there was someone who'd never denied her biological urges, Sigrid thought wryly. Hilda had married her college sweetheart in a Lutheran ceremony, but for all the attention they'd paid to birth control they could have been devout Catholics. Five children, the youngest ready to start kindergarten, and Hilda had come up pregnant again last year.

They'd had a cookout on the beach, and as the sun sank behind them and the children gathered more driftwood to feed the smoky bonfire, Sigrid could almost picture herself in a version of Hilda's life. The baby, named Lars for her favorite great-uncle, lay sleepily against her shoulder, smelling of milk and baby powder and sunshine.

She was wearing an old shirt over her bathing suit and there was a not-unpleasant tingle across her face and shoulders from too much sun. Her hair, freed from its tight knot, hung down in a single loose braid which little Lars had entangled in his chubby infant fingers. Waves ruffled the shoreline, the baby moved, and Sigrid's arms tightened around his small warm body. "Never to have this of my own?" she thought, and suddenly felt bereft.

Then two of the older children began fighting over who'd poked whom with a piece of driftwood and whether the first poke had been accidental or deliberate.

"Mo-omm!" they both called.

"I'm hungry, Mommy," said the eight-year-old, who'd eaten three hot dogs and two ears of corn less than forty-five minutes before. Her twin sister, devourer of too many potato chips and root beers, looked faintly green. "My tummy hurts," she moaned.

"Daddy," said the six-year-old. "I gotta go potty."

Five shrill voices demanding justice, revenge, or bodily nurture made the baby begin to whimper.

"Oh, Lord," sighed Hilda. Her husband took a deep swig of his scotch before wading in, and Sigrid thought longingly of her quiet Manhattan apartment.

Captain McKinnon paused in Lieutenant Harald's doorway and realized instantly that she was daydreaming. It was the first time the gruff man had caught her off guard and he was surprised how like her mother she suddenly looked. That softness now present in her wide gray eyes recalled the softness Anne's eyes had once held.

Held still?

He'd lost a partner and he'd lost Anne that day he and Leif Harald had tried to flush a killer from a sleazy hotel. Anne had blamed him for her husband's death and had cut him out of her life without a second's regret. She could not forgive him for being the one to walk away unwounded, for not being the one carried out on a stretcher with a sheet over his face.

"Murderer!" she'd sobbed when he tried to explain, to justify. "I never want to see another policeman as long as I live," she told him. "Especially you."

He wondered how she felt about having her daughter follow in Leif's footsteps. Was she still bitter? At least she hadn't poisoned the girl's mind against him. In the year or so that Lieutenant Harald had been assigned to his department, McKinnon had come to realize that Anne must never have mentioned his name. Not by the merest flicker of expression had the young policewoman shown that she knew her boss had once been her father's partner.

He saw Sigrid Harald's eyes suddenly focus on him, and all softness fled. She came to her feet immediately despite his motion to stay seated. Theirs was a strictly professional relationship and he listened intently as she described the status of the Gladwell investigation and two or three other cases that were winding down routinely.

When she'd finished, he nodded brusquely and growled, "Better get moving now, Harald. You're going to be late."

"Late?"

"There in your In basket," he said. "I was passing your door when the phone rang about an hour ago, so I took the message. He said it was important. Almost a matter of life and death."

His tone was ironic and Sigrid flushed as she read Roman Tramegra's message. Written on a departmental message sheet were a nearby address, a time, and the words *"Be there"* which McKinnon had underscored twice. She could imagine how Roman must have sounded to the captain.

"You've got thirteen minutes," McKinnon observed.

CHAPTER XIII

Although the address at which Roman Tramegra wanted her to meet him was only a dozen or so blocks northwest of headquarters, Sigrid took a cab instead of walking. She was undoubtedly going to be late, but a cab would mollify Roman. A cab would show she had tried.

Crosstown traffic was light at this hour, though, and she decided to ignore the driver's heavy foot on the accelerator. They raced through side streets shimmering with late afternoon heat and exceeded the speed limit so grossly that she was only three minutes late. That was practically like being on time.

Roman hurried forward as she paid the fare. Effusive in his pleasure, he chattered and babbled in a steady stream of italicized verbosity.

"You *did* get my message! How wonderful! I was *so* afraid that the person who answered your phone—really, my dear, shouldn't a switchboard operator or whatever he was have *some* training in the social courtesies? It just proves that all jobs shouldn't be unisexed. Women answer telephones so much more *nicely*."

"That was my boss, Roman."

"All the more reason for him to set a good example."

He pulled her across the sultry sidewalk to the corner building, a three-story brick structure. On the bottom

floor was a now-defunct butcher shop and Schnitzler's
Viennese Pastries. A sign on the door announced, *Closed
for Alterations—Grand Opening August 1*.

Roman rapped on the main glass door and it was presently opened by a middle-aged, stoop-shouldered man.

"Lieutenant Harald," said Tramegra in basso profundo
tones, "this is Mr. Stefan Schnitzler, pastry chef *par
excellence*. His sacher torte will melt in your mouth. His
topfenstrudel is the ambrosia of paradise. The daintiest
heifers of New Jersey send the fruits of their udders to
this Austrian genius and he transforms them into *Na-
poléon-schnitten* that are so thick with cream, your eyes
get fat merely gazing upon them!"

The object of this extravagant praise gave Sigrid an
embarrassed smile and held out a soft hand. Stefan
Schnitzler was two generations removed from Vienna,
and at the moment his thick brush hair was white from
plaster dust, not flour. He wore coveralls instead of an
apron to oversee the remodeling of his building. Schnitzler explained that business was so good, they'd decided
to expand into the butcher shop next door, knocking
down the wall between to provide a dining area where
customers could order coffee and eat those heavenly pastries on the spot.

"My sons and I, we're putting in new ovens in the
kitchen, new refrigerator display cases out here, and
we're going to take out some of the old walls and put
glass all around so the customers can watch us make our
pastries," he told Sigrid.

Even as he spoke, a young blond man, one of Mr.
Schnitzler's three sons, swung his sledgehammer enthusiastically and sent a shower of plaster and brick across
the store.

"Go easy, Kurt!" cried his father. The youth grinned
and settled into softer blows.

The whole Schnitzler family seemed involved in the
alterations, from a Schnitzler grandson who soaped the
windows to prevent passersby from looking in, to Schnitzler daughters-in-law who were giving the stair railings
in the entryway next door a second coat of white enamel.

"Be careful of your clothes," the baker warned as they

walked up to the vacancy Roman had discovered by chance when he had stopped in to buy pastries earlier that afternoon.

Leading them upstairs, Schnitzler explained that he and his wife and the families of his two married sons occupied the three apartments on the third floor. The second floor, formerly given over to storerooms for the shops below, had been remodeled so that his youngest son could have a small bachelor efficiency. The remaining space had been rearranged into a new, more functional storage area and a comfortable two-bedroom apartment.

"It's just perfect, isn't it?" crowed Roman; and the closer Sigrid examined the rooms, the more hopeful she became. Everything had been painted a gleaming white.

"Undercoats," said Mr. Schnitzler. "You tell them what colors you like and my girls will give the walls another coat this weekend."

Such sweet reasonableness, after years of dealing with an impersonal rental office, made Sigrid suddenly realize the advantages of a mom-and-pop operation.

The rooms were large and airy. No central air conditioning, but because of corner windows on two sides there was good cross-ventilation. She opened closets and cabinets perfunctorily, turned spigots on and off, looked into the oven and refrigerator, knowing all the time that if the asking price was anywhere near her range, she would take it.

Mr. Schnitzler was almost apologetic as he announced the figure. Roman started to haggle, but Sigrid was already pulling out her checkbook. It was only a few dollars more than what she was currently paying. She could walk to work and save the difference in transportation. Best of all, the trauma of moving would soon be over.

She wrote out a check for the sizable deposit almost happily.

Roman Tramegra beamed at them both in satisfaction of a job well done. Only now, he remembered, he'd have to start looking for a place of his own.

CHAPTER XIV

Sigrid Harald was not a morning person. Training, moral discipline and two cups of strong black coffee usually got her to work on time, but whenever she was off she seldom arose before noon. With her head buried beneath two pillows, she could sleep through sunlight, fire alarms, even Roman Tramegra's culinary clatter.

On Saturday morning, though, it was only a few minutes past seven when she sat bolt upright in bed, pricked by subconscious reminders that Oscar Nauman would be calling for her in a little over twelve hours—seven hundred and twenty minutes—and she still had no suitable dress.

"Assess the situation logically," she thought, lying back on the pillow and gazing at the ceiling. There was one long dress in her closet: a dark red velvet with sleeves that belled above the wrists and were underlined with white lace ruffles. It was a present from Grandmother Lattimore, given to her when she and Anne went down for a formal Christmas party in Carolina last year, and Sigrid rather liked it but red velvet was hardly suitable for a hot July evening.

Briefly she considered her mother's closet and for the five hundredth time wished she weren't six inches taller than Anne Harald. Her mother loved clothes and had a generous selection for all seasons. If only she were short enough to plunder Anne's closet!

"But I'm not," she reminded herself and thought about Hilda, an even dumber example of wishful thinking since Hilda was three inches shorter and twenty pounds curvier.

By logical progression, though, the thought of one cousin brought another to mind.

Strictly speaking, Kate Honeycutt was not a true cousin, only a cousin by marriage. Like most Southerners of hierarchic traditions, Anne Harald could rattle off degrees of kinship to the nth generation, but Sigrid could never keep the bloodlines straight. It was enough to know that Anne Harald and Jake Honeycutt were first or second cousins and that Jake's wife Kate was tall and thin like Sigrid except that she curved in all the right places and moved with a grace Sigrid could never hope to emulate. More to the point, Kate had been a fashion model and surely had dozens of dresses. Best of all, Kate wouldn't make a big deal out of it.

With a feeling that her problem was almost solved, Sigrid rolled over and consulted her address book for their Manhattan number. In a few moments she was speaking to a sleepy Kate Honeycutt.

"Who the devil calls at such an ungodly hour?" Jake Honeycutt asked with a yawn.

"Sigrid," answered Kate, running a fingernail across the ridge of his bare shoulder. "Sigrid Harald. She's coming over later to borrow a long dress."

"One of *yours*?" Somehow it was difficult to imagine the angular body of his cool, reserved cousin in one of Kate's dresses.

"Of course one of mine, silly. We're built almost exactly alike."

"Heresy," said Jake, smiling up at Kate. "Nobody's built like you."

Even after two and a half years of marriage, it was still a thing of wonder to wake up with so much sweet loveliness beside him. "You're not ready to get up yet, are you?" he asked, reaching for her.

• • •

Roman Tramegra was surprised when Sigrid entered the kitchen and he glanced automatically at the digital clock over the refrigerator.

7:30.

The clock also confirmed that it was Saturday, as he had thought.

"Are you well?" he asked doubtfully, looking at her robe and bare feet.

Normally she appeared from her room each morning fully dressed, her hair firmly pinned in place. Today she wore a white robe of cool Egyptian cotton, one of the exotic djellebas her mother had sent her while on a Middle Eastern assignment. The yoke was heavily embroidered and her dark hair swirled loosely around her thin face.

"I'm fine," she answered. "The coffee smells wonderful."

"Sit there, my dear, and let me pour. It's Jamaica Blue Mountain. Would you believe our little deli around the corner carries Jamaica Blue Mountain? Try a pastry, too," he urged, pushing a plate of tarts and jam-filled croissants toward her. "Not as good as Schnitzler's, but adequate. Quite adequate."

Sigrid looked at the large soft man with something very near affection; it came to her that she would probably miss the rumble of his deep-voiced monologues, his enthusiasms over small details, yes, even his magpie curiosity about her cases. She bit into a peach croissant and, knowing how it would please him, began to tell of finding Penelope Naughton and Elena Dorato in the middle of her current homicide.

"Penelope Naughton!" he sighed and immediately quoted a slightly rude but very witty limerick the Naughty Penny had written in the twenties, which Sigrid had never heard.

She laughed out loud at its punch line and Roman, pleasantly gratified, smoothed a strand of light brown hair over his bald spot and confided, "When I was a child, I wanted desperately to be a member of the New York literati, the smart set.

"I was twelve the first time my parents let me come with them to New York. I *begged* them to book rooms at the Algonquin, but they'd always stayed at the Plaza and where they'd always stayed is from whence they would never stray. I was simply *furious* and even though I didn't know a *thing* about the city, I ran straight out and didn't stop running till I got to the Algonquin."

"Did you expect them to still be there?" Sigrid asked sympathetically. "Benchley, Parker, Naughton and all the rest?"

"Oh, no. I knew they were either dead or scattered. In the flesh wasn't important. It was enough just to sit in the Oak Room and stare at the Round Table itself and imagine how it was. And to pretend that if I'd been born a few years earlier, I'd have been one of them."

He stirred another spoonful of sugar into his coffee. "I was quite disappointed by a Dorothy Parker interview a year or so before she died. It was on radio, one of Richard Lamparski's whatever-became-of-so-and-so? She sounded dreadfully bitter and depressed about the way her life had turned out, as if the Round Table had been partly to blame. She said it was all a sham—that they weren't very brilliant or even very nice—that they were only a bunch of smart-alecks showing off. Even if it was true, she shouldn't have said it."

"Did she happen to tell why Penelope Naughton dropped out?"

"No, just that Penny may really have been the brightest after all because she left at the height of things and kept her mouth shut forever after.

"Ah, well," he said lightly. "The moving finger writes and all that. And so you have the golden Elena, too? That *is* a combination—Penelope Naughton's brains and Elena Dorato's beauty. Are they connected?"

"I doubt it. Naughton became a recluse almost thirty years before Dorato killed herself."

"You know, *Cinderella*'s going to be on television one night this week," said Roman. "They usually show it only around Christmas. Do you suppose it has anything to do with the auction?"

"Auction?"

"At Satterthwaite's Wednesday. They're auctioning off the real glass slippers."

Sigrid looked blank and Roman, ever a fund of trivial information, was happy to explain.

"It was before your time, my dear, so perhaps you never heard. There were at least two pairs of glass slippers made for the movie, maybe more because I seem to recall that they broke a couple on the set. The Lord High Chamberlain cut his palm rather badly on one that simply shattered in his hand. There were duplicates because they had to have a tiny set for the ugly stepsisters to try on—you remember the close-ups when they can't even get their big toes in?—and there was another pair for Elena Dorato to wear. The gossip columnists *swore* they were size ten. She did have large feet for such a lovely body, poor creature.

"Anyhow, it's the pair she wore herself that's being auctioned off. They should bring several thousand. Shall we go and bid?"

"Sorry," Sigrid smiled, holding her cup out for more coffee, "but I blew my entire shoe allowance on that apartment deposit yesterday."

Nevertheless, she wondered about that auction Wednesday. Who was the current owner of those slippers and was it only a coincidence that they were being sold a few days after Clayton Gladwell's murder?

CHAPTER XV

"Look," said Marian Tildon, pushing back a tumble of auburn hair with her free hand. "Would you just *go?*"

The carrot-haired infant clutched in her other arm screamed with anger and tried to twist free.

"At least let me help you put the playpen in the yard," said Tillie, who felt guilty knowing his youngest was crying because she felt abandoned by him.

"She'll be fine as soon as you're out of sight," Marian said callously, but she relented and handed the red-faced baby over to her husband.

"Sh-sh, my sweetling," Tillie crooned while Marian competently maneuvered the playpen through the utility room and out into their tiny backyard. She wore white shorts and a strapless tube top; despite four children she was still a perfect size eight, a fact Tillie could note with pleasure even while Jenny howled in his ear. The baby's screams modulated into sobs and gradually died away as Tillie patted her back in comforting rhythm.

An ailanthus tree in the next yard stretched its branches over the picket fence, blocking out some of the hot morning sun, and Marian set the playpen in its shade. The day promised to be another scorcher and the baby's bright orange hair already curled in tight damp ringlets across her head. She started to whimper again when Tillie set her inside the pen, but he quickly pulled out a clean handkerchief and said, "Where's my mouse? Did you see my mouse?"

Jenny's lower lip quivered and her large green eyes puddled with tears, but she watched Tillie twist and knot the handkerchief into a shape vaguely suggesting a small animal.

"Nice mouse," said Tillie, squatting down so the infant could see through the playpen's net side. He pretended to stroke his creation with one hand while making it jiggle with the fingers of the other hand. A flip of his middle finger sent the "mouse" somersaulting into the air. "Whoops! Come back here, mouse!"

Jenny gurgled with laughter and Tillie made a great show of scrambling through the grass to look for the errant creature.

Marian smiled and turned in time to intercept three-year-old Carl as he burst through the doorway. She scooped him up easily and carried him back inside.

"I wanna see the mouse!" he told her indignantly as she plunked him down on a tall kitchen stool.

"Have some juice," she said, filling his blue plastic mug along with Jenny's bottle. The television in the living room went from cartoons to commercials and the two older children raced into the kitchen.

The way their ears were attuned to its openings and closings, the refrigerator door might as well have a cowbell tied to it, thought Marian, and poured two more mugs of juice.

"When's Dad coming in?" asked Chuck. His face was as freckled as those of his three younger siblings, but he was the only one with his father's sandy hair, round chin, and earnest blue eyes.

"As soon as he can get away from Jenny."

She screwed the nipple and cap on the plastic bottle of juice and told Carl to stay with Chuck and Shelly. "Daddy and I'll be right back," she promised.

It took several minutes to switch Jenny's interest from the handkerchief mouse to her bottle, but once she lay down to drink it, her attention was captured by the sway-

ing tree branches overhead and Tillie was able to slip
away unnoticed into the house where Carl was having
second thoughts about staying home.

He knew walking across a long hot bridge didn't sound
like much fun. On the other hand, he darkly suspected
that he might be missing something if Shelly and Chuck
went with Daddy and he didn't.

In the end, cartoons, the reminder that he'd been
invited to go splash in a friend's wading pool, and the
promise of a game of catch after supper persuaded him
to stay; and Tillie followed Chuck and Shelly out to the
car in good conscience.

At Brooklyn Heights he left the children exploring the
Promenade, a cantilevered esplanade built over two lev-
els of traffic and the piers far below. Commanding a
spectacular view of the harbor and lower Manhattan, it
was about a third of a mile long, partially shaded by tall
trees, and so well frequented by joggers and strollers
that Tillie felt safe leaving Chuck and Shelly with only
the usual instructions not to bother anyone or wander
from the Promenade.

"And if somebody says they've come to take us to you,
we don't believe 'em," said Chuck before his father could
finish. "Right?"

"Right," Tillie smiled.

Dr. Morarji Bhattacherjea opened the door before the
bell finished ringing and Tillie wondered whether the
radiologist had been waiting for him all morning.

He had found Dr. Ishrad Bhattacherjea's English
stilted and heavily accented yesterday. Her husband's
was more precisely correct; his slight accent was one
Tillie associated with East Indian colonials. Of Pakistani
birth, Dr. Bhattacherjea was two or three inches shorter
than Tillie with light brown skin, dark hair combed
straight back, a bland smile and a certain cautiousness
in his heavy-lidded eyes.

He ushered Tillie into a room furnished in heavy opu-
lence. Patterned Kashmir rugs lay atop wall-to-wall carpeting, and the couches and chairs were overstuffed
velours in muted greens and purples. Cooking odors had

drifted through the apartment and the smell of unfamiliar spices hung in the air. Unfamiliar, but appetizing. They reminded Tillie that it would soon be lunchtime.

"My wife said you wish to discuss our connection with Mr. Gladwell?" said Dr. Bhattacherjea, offering Tillie a box of thin brown cigarettes.

Tillie declined the cigarettes and settled into a deep armchair, his notebook comfortably on his knee. "You know that Mr. Gladwell was murdered night before last?"

"Yes. Someone at the hospital saw it in the newspaper and remembered that he was in for tests this past spring."

"You were his doctor?"

"Oh no, no." The doctor made a deprecatory denial with his hands as he tipped his cigarette into a gleaming brass ashtray. "Dr. Josephus Galtman was his physician; I merely did the X rays and fluoroscopes Dr. Galtman requested."

"But you did become friendly?" Tillie persisted. "I understand he did you a favor—helped with a niece's papers or something?"

Again the denial with his small hands. "Not exactly a favor, Officer Tildon. A favor is usually for free, is it not? Mr. Gladwell did procure for us some necessary papers, but I assure you that we reimbursed him. At his regular rates."

"In cash? In installments?"

"Even with checking accounts and credit cards, cash is still legal tender in America," Dr. Bhattacherjea smiled. "And Mr. Gladwell was kind enough to let us break his fee into manageable payments."

"You have receipts, of course?"

The doctor gave an apologetic shrug. "Alas, no. I'm afraid we are not very businesslike. My accountant gets very angry with my wife and me, always no receipts."

"According to his office manager, you were to have seen Gladwell again on Monday?"

"Yes, a final payment to end our association," Bhattacherjea said smoothly.

Tillie consulted his notes. "That would make nine

hundred dollars you would have paid just to straighten out a minor bureaucratic snarl."

"Perhaps that seems excessive to you, Sergeant Tildon, but not to me. For my wife's peace of mind . . ." he smiled again, appealing to Tillie's understanding of the price one must sometimes pay for domestic tranquillity.

"We're not entirely clear exactly what it was that Gladwell did about your niece."

"Her visitor's visa had expired and Mr. Gladwell was able to get it changed to a student visa."

"She must be finding life in New York a big change. Has she been here long?"

"Two years."

For some reason, that surprised Tillie. "She didn't seem to understand English when I spoke to her yesterday."

"No, she speaks it poorly. I fear Halima may be backward for her age, but she tries hard and she is very good with my little sons."

In his longest burst of volubility yet, Dr. Bhattacherjea volunteered the information that the child wasn't really a niece. "Only the daughter of my wife's cousin, a branch of the family that has come down in the world, you understand. My wife felt the shame of their poverty and pitied her cousin. She has a kindly heart and persuaded me to let her help at least one of the children."

He described the African village from which they had rescued the child Halima: the primitive sanitation, the depressed economy, the high rate of illiteracy. "Here she has a bed of her own," he boasted, "new clothes, a modern home."

"And a good education?" said Tillie. He and Marian lived in a less affluent section of Brooklyn, but even though Chuck and Shelly's school was old and poorly equipped, their teachers seemed to be holding the line on educational standards. A Brooklyn Heights public school probably offered many more extras.

"I suppose she goes to the school over on Dawson Avenue. Does she like it?"

"Oh yes, very much," said Dr. Bhattacherjea. He glanced pointedly at the heavy gold watch on his wrist.

Ignoring the hint even though his eyes were beginning to sting from the cigarettes the doctor was chain-smoking in the unventilated room, Tillie checked through his notes once more and decided he might as well tackle the man head on.

He chose his words carefully to describe Gladwell's double filing system and the hidden notebooks from his apartment.

"So when we find your name attached to a blue folder in his office and notations in a secret account book of cash payments you have made, we have to wonder if he was blackmailing you and your wife as well," he finished.

For the first time, Bhattacherjea's eyes darted away from Tillie's and his bland urbanity seemed to slip. He moistened his thin lips and lit another of those endless brown cigarettes before finally looking at Tillie with a fatalistic expression in his hooded eyes.

"You did not believe what I said before. You think I lied. You are right. But it is not easy to tell a policeman the entire truth. You wonder why we paid Mr. Gladwell cash and why his fee was so high? It was because there was an irregularity in Halima's papers—nothing illegal, you understand, only a technicality. But someone in Immigration had to be bribed to overlook it. One cannot pay *baksheesh* with a personal check."

The doctor's embarrassed tone was right and his confession certainly explained the blue folder, but Tillie smelled a distinct odor of red herring. Nevertheless, he was courteous as he asked Dr. Bhattacherjea if he would account for his and his wife's whereabouts on Thursday afternoon.

"My wife assisted in an operation until six o'clock, and I worked in my lab till five."

He named two or three people to whom he'd spoken when he left for the day. Tillie decided he might just have been able to make it from the hospital to Gladwell's office in time to shoot the lawyer around five-thirty, but that would be cutting it rather close.

He shut his notebook and thanked Dr. Bhattacherjea

for his cooperation. Perhaps he should have insisted on speaking to Dr. Ishrad Bhattacherjea again, but her alibi should be easy to confirm and he suspected she would add nothing without her husband's approval.

Anyhow, the heavy cigarette smoke combined with those spicy cooking aromas had given him a mild headache.

Even though the day had grown appreciatively hotter while he was upstairs, Tillie was glad to get back outside to fresh air.

The Bhattacherjea apartment had felt hermetically sealed from the elements and muffled against any outside sounds. One would never guess that three little boys and a young girl were somewhere in the apartment's depths laughing and squabbling as all children do.

Tillie walked down the steps from Clark Street onto the Promenade and thought how good it was to be outdoors in sunshine and noise. He spotted Shelly's bright red hair in the distance, then picked out Chuck's blue Mets shirt just as the children saw him.

He pocketed his notebook, dismissed all thought of murder and motives from his mind, and beamed as his son and daughter raced toward him.

CHAPTER XVI

In the hastily straightened bedroom, Kate Honeycutt looked at Jake's cousin critically and decided that there was hope for that young woman after all. It was the first time she'd seen Sigrid stripped, and though she hadn't given any thought to the subject before, it would not have surprised Kate to see tailored police blue underwear.

She was heartened to discover that under a truly hideous black knit shirt and beige slacks, Sigrid Harald wore delicate lace bra and panties. And even though she was thin, she wasn't quite as skinny as those baggy clothes would lead one to believe.

"You're wasted in police work," said Kate. "You should be modeling lingerie."

"*Ja, ja,*" Sigrid said in a self-conscious Oley Olsen accent. "I dreamed I discovered who done it in my Maidenform bra?"

"You could. You're built for it."

"You sound like my mother. Next you'll be talking about my wonderful bones."

"Anne has a good eye," Kate grinned, "but okay, I'll stop embarrassing you."

She folded back her closet doors. "What's the occasion again?"

Sigrid was fascinated by Kate's closet. It took up two whole walls and everything was arranged by season and occasion. "It's a benefit ball for the Museum of Modern Art."

"In *July*? I thought it was against the law to have anything like that before September."

"I wouldn't know," said Sigrid. "I've never gone to one before and if I had any sense, I'd call Nauman and cancel out of this one."

"You'll do no such thing!"

Kate had given up modeling for fabric design, and although she was competent in her field, she had no illusions about its aesthetics. As a commercial artist she was doing quite well, but she kept up with what fine artists were doing and had great respect for Oscar Nauman's work. A little of his glamour spilled over to Sigrid, though Kate would have lent a dress just as willingly had Sigrid been spending the evening with John Q. Public.

She liked Jake's shy, awkward cousin and, along with several younger members of the family, thought Sigrid had physical possibilities if she could only cultivate a less negative image of herself. Kate decided it would be a grand coup if she were the one to finally wave a magic wand and transform the family's ugly duckling into a swan.

So she pulled out satin gowns, taffeta knickers, and gauzy palazzo pants until the bed and floor were strewn with colors and fabrics. "God, what a bunch of junk I've held onto!" she said.

Since marrying Jake, she seldom wore the high-powered fashions for which she'd once been noted. For every frock pulled out, another was left in the closet, vetoed as to ruffled, too outré, too revealing. There was a white jersey that clung nicely to Sigrid's lean body, but the front was a split halter that crossed over the breasts and exposed her midriff.

"Once you start dancing, that's not all it exposes," Kate warned.

Sigrid agreed that she preferred a dress she wouldn't have to tug at all evening, something that would stay in place by itself.

She was zipped and trussed into several that caught Kate's eye, but she became less hopeful as the contents of the closet dwindled.

"What's that one?" she asked of a dress Kate had flipped past.

"That?" Kate paused and frowned at the garment in question. "I never liked this color on me"—Kate had honey-brown hair and blue-green eyes—"but maybe on you . . ."

"Forget it," said Sigrid, when she saw how the dress was constructed. "It doesn't have a back. How would I keep it on? With glue?"

Kate laughed and helped her slip into it. From the front, the sleeveless long dress seemed a simple summer cotton, small black-and-white checks on semisheer handkerchief linen. It had a deep flounce with a plain white under ruffle. The wide square neckline, cut just below the collarbone, was edged with a crisply tucked white ruffle about an inch or so wide that went straight back over the shoulders and continued down the back. Except for that narrow ruffle and an equally narrow strip of checked fabric on either side, the dress had no back at all above the waist.

And, as Sigrid had feared, the moment she moved, the dress slid apart.

"Wait," said Kate. "This goes with it."

Draped across the hanger was what looked like a long shoelace of rolled white batiste and Kate threaded it through unseen loops at the edge of the ruffled sides. It crisscrossed Sigrid's slender back twice and tied with a bow at the small of her back.

That simple lacing turned a chaste frock into something spicier, implying that a gentle tug of the bow's free end would unloose all sorts of delicious possibilities.

"I don't know," said Sigrid, frowning at her reflection as she turned before the mirror.

"It's perfect!" Kate caroled.

And it was. The square neckline balanced Sigrid's long neck and the black-and-white checks echoed her slate-gray eyes. The full skirt and deep flounces even bestowed an automatic grace to her movements.

"Is Oscar Nauman tall enough for you to wear heels?"

Sigrid nodded and Kate made her try on black patent-leather slippers that were nothing more than a three-inch heel and thin straps across instep and ankle. They were a perfect fit.

"Gloves," said Kate, rummaging for long white ones.

"Does anybody still wear white gloves?" asked Sigrid, remembering the formality of long-ago dancing classes.

"You can start a new trend," Kate said firmly. "Earrings."

She clipped clusters of dangling pearls on Sigrid's ears, loosened a couple of tendrils of hair around her face, and before Sigrid could object, called Jake in for his opinion.

The lanky, Southern-born stockbroker entered that feminine chaos with a broad grin and Sigrid faced him in a flush of embarrassment, her chin high because she loathed being stared at.

"You look marvelous," he said, and the sincerity in his tone was a gratifying antidote to Sigrid's self-consciousness.

Jake shook his head, wondering why he'd never noticed what elegant facial planes his cousin possessed. Down South, among the Lattimore women, she had always been overshadowed by their petite prettiness. How had he missed looking beneath the surface? And that dress, with its devastating blend of innocence and sensuality . . .

"Whoever's taking you out tonight's gonna be driven crazy by the contradiction, honey," he drawled. "You look like a schoolteacher from the front and a honky-tonk angel from behind!" He grinned at his wife. "How come you never wore that dress for me, Katydid?"

The intimate look that passed between them made Sigrid suddenly awkward again. She pulled off the gloves and earrings and reached for her street clothes, feeling a bit like Cinderella after the clock struck midnight.

And that reminded her: she really mustn't forget to have someone look into the Satterthwaite auction Wednesday, see who else was abandoning Cinderella trappings.

• • •

At the Lantana Walk Nursing Home over in Queens, William Burchlow waited while the new man, Higgins, changed the bed linen for an elderly patient, shifting the invalid from one side of the bed to the other with a gentleness at odds with his beefy hands and ugly face.

Good help, at the minimum wages Mr. Burchlow preferred to pay, was hard to find; nevertheless, the director did not believe in overlooking slackness, so when Higgins walked past him with his hands full of soiled linen, Mr. Burchlow followed him out to the hall.

"One moment, please, Higgins."

The stocky orderly turned and looked at this employer with an unpleasant tightening of his crooked mouth. "Something wrong?"

"No, no. Your work is, in the main, quite satisfactory, Higgins, but perhaps I didn't make myself quite clear on one point."

"Yeah?"

"It's about yesterday. One of our patients was needlessly bothered."

Higgins looked sullen, but Mr. Burchlow plunged on. "I told you when I hired you last month that you must keep an eye out for strangers walking in off the street. Particularly when they intrude upon clients who have had no outside contact in several years. There's Dussel, Scocozza, Forthingay, and Spiropolis on your floor. Those four have outlived all their friends or relatives and they are out of touch with reality; so when a stranger suddenly appears in their rooms, they become confused and disoriented. You let a total stranger into Mr. Dussel's room yesterday, Higgins. Fortunately he wasn't there long enough to cause any trouble, but he could have, Higgins. He could have.

"In the future, I shall expect you to be more aware of who's wandering around your floor when you're on duty. Is that clear?"

"Dussel, Scocozza, Forthingay, Spiropolis. No visitors. Right." Higgins stuffed the dirty linen into the basket of his cart and moved on to the next room without waiting to be dismissed.

Mr. Burchlow was annoyed. With unemployment running to double digits, he thought, why can't I find competent help with more docile temperaments?

The thought of docile natures brought his receptionist to mind. Little Rosa, with her soft round face, her firm young bottom, her wraparound skirt that was always coming unwrapped when she leaned across the counter. He decided he might as well go down and see if she'd finished compiling those figures he'd asked for.

He would have been quite indignant if he'd known that at that very moment the evil-looking Higgins had Rosa on his mind, too.

CHAPTER XVII

I

Sigrid's afternoon became curiously schizoid. Roman Tramegra had a late lunch waiting and was immensely interested both in her dress and in the preparations he thought she should make for a formal evening. Kate had sent her home with makeup, curling iron and bright red fingernail polish, none of which Sigrid had ever used before but which Kate had made her promise to try.

"She's quite right," said Roman when Sigrid made a disparaging remark about painting herself. "With a black-and-white dress, you *must* have little touches of red to perk it up."

He looked at her slender hands critically. "Of course, you *will* have to reshape your nails."

"What's wrong with them?" They looked all right to her, slightly longer than her fingertips and neatly rounded.

"Your cuticles need attention and the nails themselves should be more pointed to add an illusion of length. If you'll get your manicure set, I'll show you what I mean."

Sigrid confessed that her manicure set consisted of nail clippers and a metal file, so Roman brought out his own scissors, orange sticks, and emery boards. Soon she was seated at the kitchen table feeling slightly foolish with both hands soaking in a dish of warm soapy water. When the telephone rang, she tucked it between ear and shoulder and continued to soak her nails as Tillie described his interview with Dr. Morarji Bhattacherjea.

"Bribery payments to an immigration official?" she said skeptically. "If he's making it up, he seems to have thought of everything."

"It even explains his cash payments to Gladwell," Tillie agreed. "Could be true, I suppose. I'll send someone to check the kid's school records. And the Bhattacherjeas' alibis, too, of course."

"Of course," said Sigrid, watching Roman push back her cuticles with an orange stick. As a rule she hated to be touched, but Roman's avuncular manner kept it impersonal. In fact, his ministrations were almost soothing.

Even so, she was not allowed to give herself up to sybaritic pleasures entirely. She had left instructions the evening before, and her phone continued to ring throughout the afternoon as reports trickled in of alibis checked and confirmed.

While Roman applied a second coat of enamel to her nails Sigrid learned that, yes, Nancy Kuipers had been seen in the audience of her daughter's four o'clock dance recital. Several of the waiters at the Chinese restaurant agreed that mother and daughter had eaten dinner there afterward. The little girl was a whiz with chopsticks so they remembered her very clearly. At five-thirty, the estimated time of Gladwell's murder, they were probably just beginning their bowls of hot-and-sour soup.

Millicent Barr said she had been met downstairs a few minutes before five by a pilot with Global Airlines. She had first dropped those two checks, one from Justin Trent and the other from a Texas firm, in the bank's night deposit slot. Afterward they had gone for drinks at a nearby tavern, to dinner at a midtown restaurant and then back to the receptionist's apartment. The tavern had been crowded and, while the bartender remembered Milly Barr, he couldn't swear that she hadn't slipped out for the fifteen or twenty minutes it might have taken her to return to the office. The pilot would be questioned when he returned from Bombay on Monday.

As for Jean Parrish, Gladwell's incurious secretary lived one block from the Grant City station on Staten Island. Five days a week she left the office no later than five, took a subway to Battery Park, the ferry to Staten Island, then the train to Grant City.

Sigrid unbraided her hair and brushed it vigorously while Detective Elaine Albee told how Jean Parrish's neighbors swore that clocks could be set by the secretary's commuting habits. She had been seen coming home at the usual time on Thursday afternoon, and Albee thought a half hour's difference would have been noticed.

Sigrid was fresh from her shower and her hair was neatly rebraided into its usual knot when Detective Lowry called just before seven. While she concentrated on his report and how his findings fitted into the overall picture, Roman took advantage of her preoccupation to loosen tendrils of dark hair and set to work with Kate Honeycutt's curling iron.

One of the guards at the Pierpont Morgan Library, two blocks north of Gladwell's office building, remembered that Justin Trent had been there Thursday afternoon. The financier visited the library frequently enough to be a familiar face, and the guard recalled holding the door for him to leave about ten minutes before closing time at five. From there, Lowry had walked first to the Public Library at Forty-second and Fifth and thence to Trent's townhouse in the East Sixties.

"The total distance is about two miles," said Lowry. "Two miles an hour certainly isn't breaking any records. On the other hand, it *was* rush hour and the sidewalks were clogged. I did it in thirty-five minutes, but an hour's probably about right for a guy his age."

Jim Lowry spoke with the unconscious superiority a man of twenty-six feels for a man thirty years older.

Sigrid hung up and was making a few notes on her pad when it suddenly penetrated that Roman was flourishing a large pair of scissors and murmuring about a few snips here and a few snips there. She drew back, picked up a hand mirror lying nearby and was horrified to see a row of long tight curls dangling from the hairline all around her head like a rack of corkscrews set out for sale.

"*Roman!*"

"It's because they're too long," he said confidently. "When I trim them, they'll just wisp around your hairline. You'll see."

"Absolutely not!" she said firmly. Her newly painted fingers flew through her hair, unpinning and unbraiding.

"Then let me put your hair up properly," he pleaded. "No cutting, I promise. And if you don't like it, you can put it back the way it was."

Reluctantly, Sigrid sat still while he brushed her hair out and began afresh. When he finished twenty minutes later, she looked at her reflection doubtfully.

He had coiled it into an elegant twist on top of her head and teased a little fullness into either side of her temples.

"It won't slide down, will it?" she asked fearfully.

Patiently, Roman pushed in another half-dozen hairpins till Sigrid felt secure. "Most women use hair spray," he said pointedly.

She had meant to be ready when Oscar Nauman arrived, but lacing up the back of that dress proved trickier than she'd expected. She refused to call Roman for help and was still struggling with getting the loops of the bow even when the doorbell rang. From her room, she heard the bass rumble of Roman's voice mingle with Nauman's baritone and was suddenly stricken with stage fright. Her back to the mirror, she scowled over her shoulder at the picture she made.

"Bare back, ruffles, and my hair will probably fall down as soon as I start dancing and how in God's name can I have wasted a whole day getting ready for this stupid evening?" she thought angrily.

She jerked the bow tight, clipped on the long pearl earrings and strode down the hall, the full skirt swirling around her legs, her gray eyes stormy.

Nauman and Roman both rose as she entered the living room. The white-haired artist stood well over six feet and, although he had to be around sixty, there was a vigorous youthfulness to his hard lean body. His eyes were a bright blue, clear and unsullied, the blue of an

October sky on the morning after autumn's first frost, a blue that pierced with the intensity of the brain behind it.

He held a gin and tonic Roman had made and looked perfectly at ease in his white dinner jacket, black tie and white silk shirt with gold-and-onyx studs.

In the few months that he had known her, Oscar Nauman had learned that it was best not to comment on Sigrid's appearance when her chin was at that angle and her cheeks were flushed with self-consciousness, so he handed her a drink and spoke of the hot weather instead.

Roman Tramegra was less perceptive and clucked and hovered until Sigrid rounded on him savagely when he offered to tie a neater bow.

"Damn it, Roman! Will you leave me alone? I'm tired of being fussed over. The bow's fine. It's supposed to flop like that."

Nauman suppressed a grin, but Sigrid saw the merriment in his blue eyes. She set down her glass and in an icy voice suggested that perhaps they should be leaving if he intended to get there before midnight.

"By all means," he agreed equably and said good night to Tramegra, who had a rather hurt look on his broad soft face.

Downstairs, Sigrid pushed through the glass doors ahead of Oscar and headed for his battered yellow sports car parked illegally at the curb beside a fire hydrant. Its top was down this sultry July night and she reached for the door handle, but he was before her.

"I'm perfectly capable of opening a door for myself," she snapped.

Nauman tucked the ruffled flounce of her long skirt inside, gently closed the door, then bent over and gave her a long hard kiss.

She wanted to jerk away, but his strong hands were cupped around her face and she was sharply conscious of what such a hasty movement might do to Roman's unfamiliar coiffure. For the moment, she was trapped; but when he released her, she glared straight ahead as he circled the car and slid in beside her.

"What was that for?" she asked coldly. "Am I supposed

to go all soft and dainty now, overpowered by your masterful kiss?"

"No. You're supposed to relax and accept two facts: one, I'm very pleased you came; two, you look lovely."

Sigrid went mute.

He turned the key in the ignition and eased the car out into the heavy Saturday night traffic streaming past them. Normally he drove at a speed officially designated as careless and reckless, but tonight his foot was so light on the accelerator that Sigrid's hair was barely ruffled.

They stopped at a red light and Nauman looked at her warily.

"Look, I didn't mean to insult you with courtesy. Chalk it up to the formality of black tie and evening dress. Goes with the territory. I know you can open your own doors. *Any* doors. I'm perfectly willing to admit you could probably cold-cock me in a fistfight, shoot out all the street lights with one bullet—maybe even pick up the world if Atlas shrugged. I want to take you dancing, but if you'd really rather kick a few more soft furry animals, we can make it the nearest SPCA shelter instead."

"I'm sorry," said Sigrid. "I was pretty rotten to Roman, wasn't I?"

"What about me?"

"No one ever mistook you for a soft furry animal," she said dryly.

He laughed out loud and the light turned green.

Sigrid had assumed that the affair would be booked into one of the large midtown hotels and she was surprised when Nauman headed across town to the West Side piers. For the MOMA benefit, the directors of a South American line had donated the use of one of their cruise ships for the evening, a gesture of goodwill for them (not to mention publicity and tax write-offs) and a novel setting for the ball's organizers.

The ship's ballroom had been decorated to mimic an exotic tropical forest. Masses of green foliage were enlivened by colorful silk birds and butterflies which hovered among fresh flowers. Equally colorful were the gowned and coiffured women who entered the room on the arms of formally dressed men. Expensive perfumes competed with male colognes, diamonds and dentures flashed with equal brilliance, and Nauman seemed to be greeted by name by every third person they passed.

He smiled and nodded and tossed a quip or two in return, but the orchestra was playing a wonderfully inviting waltz and he kept moving toward the dance floor, trying not to get entangled before he'd had a chance to dance with Sigrid.

"Oscar! How ya doing?" cried a jovial voice and their path was blocked by a balding man with the grin of a Jewish leprechaun. His eyes raked Sigrid with good-humored frankness. "Where did an old reprobate like you find such a stunning creature? More to the point," he said, turning to Sigrid with mock confidentiality, "how did he persuade you to be seen with him in public?"

"They still letting you out at night?" asked Nauman. "And I told her this was going to be an exclusive affair. Siga, our dishonorable mayor; Mr. Mayor, Sigrid Harald, one of New York's finest."

"I'll say she is," beamed the mayor, gallantly lifting Sigrid's hand to his lips. He paused in midair. "New York's finest? As in police? *City* police?"

Sigrid nodded and gave her rank and posting.

"Terrific!" he said as Nauman eased her away. He was promptly surrounded by three elderly bediamonded matrons, but he called a parting, "Tell ol' Mac I send regards."

"You didn't give me time to ask for a raise." Sigrid smiled as they reached the edge of the dance floor.

"Write him a letter," said Nauman and took her into his arms.

A slow foxtrot had brought even reluctant dancers onto the floor, and Sigrid soon found herself wishing they had a wide sweeping place to themselves for Nauman moved with unexpected ease and confidence. After the first wary moments of matching her steps to his, she relaxed and let him lead her through intricate patterns as the music segued into a rumba, to a tango, then into a waltz.

Oscar was delighted. In her moments of extreme self-consciousness she could become almost paralyzed with awkwardness, yet tonight she moved with a feather's grace, intuiting his moves before he made them.

Mascara made her wide gray eyes more haunting than usual, but what gave more pleasure than her unexpected glamour was the mere fact of her trying. That she who so ignored fashion and scorned beauty wiles should gloss her lips, enamel her nails and don a decidedly sexy dress for this evening with him touched Nauman deeply. He tightened his hold on her slender body and rested his cheek lightly against her soft dark hair.

For Sigrid, time was suspended. She had stopped analyzing and judging and was content merely to be. Moving in harmony to the music's rhythm was giving her something akin to the out-of-body euphoria she occasionally experienced while swimming.

To their regret, the waltz drew to an end. Bright-colored strobes kaleidoscoped across the ballroom and the bandleader cried, "Get down, people! Let's boogie!"

"Damn!" said Oscar and swept her through one of the doorways. The deck was softly lit and nearly unpeopled. They found a deserted stretch of railing and leaned upon it silently, watching the play of light on the river's ripples. Sigrid was grateful for Nauman's silence.

The night air was still warm but not unpleasant, and here on a deck high above the water there was a slight breeze. Oscar drew out one of his elaborately carved meerschaum pipes and soon the mellow aroma of aged tobacco blended with the tang of salt air.

"Shall I go look for something to drink?"

"Not yet," she said, her eyes following the lights of a tour boat out in the channel heading downstream. She wondered if they marked the blazing lights of this luxurious cruise ship and if distance softened the music that reached them.

In a similar mood, Oscar began to reminisce about various ocean voyages he'd made: his first trip to Europe in a troop transport as a very young, very scared enlistee; the last voyage of the first *Queen Elizabeth*, at the end of her glory days; on a Dutch freighter five or six years ago.

"Ah, there you are, Nauman," said a friendly mas-

culine voice behind them. "Warhol said he thought he
saw you come this way. Sorry to intrude, but Bitsy Lau-
fermann asked me to help round up the guests of honor.
They're ready to start."

The newcomer, elegantly attired in formal black evening clothes, hesitated as he recognized Nauman's com-
panion. Oscar started to introduce them, but Justin Trent
smiled easily and said, "We've already met. How nice
to see you again so soon, Lieutenant Harald."

She returned Trent's smile with a nod. Nauman looked
at her quizzically, but she chose to interpret his look as
a different question. "It's so hot inside, I'll wait for you
here," she told him.

The two men moved away and Sigrid walked a few
paces farther down the deck to where the music was less
insistent and the lights even dimmer. She tried to remember if she'd ever been on any boat besides the Staten
Island ferry or one of the Hudson River cruise boats and
decided she hadn't. The few times she'd accompanied
her mother to Europe or South America, Anne had always been in such a hurry that they'd flown. Ships were
for people with as much time to squander as money.

Elena Dorato had chosen a ship for her last trip.

Sigrid gazed down into the gently lapping water far
below. Here on *L'Espuma de Mar* anchored to a Manhattan pier, surrounded by music, lights and busy river
traffic, suicide seemed an incongruous option. But on a
dark and lonely ocean, tormented with thoughts of losing
her beauty, of growing older, perhaps fearful that a talent
for light musicals could never be stretched to cover heavy
drama—had it seemed easier just to lean further over
the rail, or had someone helped her along? Had it really
been suicide—or murder?

And what had Gladwell meant when he wrote "further
payment in kind" beside Dorato's initials in his secret
account book?

"Lieutenant?"

Sigrid whirled sharply.

"I'm so sorry," said Justin Trent from the shadows
beyond her. "I thought you heard me speak to you."

"I'm afraid my mind was elsewhere."

"Ships do that. It's easy to forget yourself out on the water." He stepped into the light, carrying two glasses of wine. "Nauman said you might like this."

"Thank you."

"Have you known him long?"

"Only a few months," she answered.

"If I'd realized yesterday that you were friends, I would have shown you some of his paintings you may not have seen."

Sigrid remembered that there had been a small abstract on the wall behind her in Trent's study. She described its position. "Was that one of Nauman's?"

"Yes, but my favorites are in the breakfast room where I can enjoy them every morning."

From the way he spoke, Sigrid gathered that he owned three or four of Nauman's pictures and she expressed surprise that he should so like a modern artist.

"I can appreciate the art of other ages, so why not my own?" asked Trent. "Aren't you just as eclectic, to like Mabuse and Nauman both?"

Most of Nauman's work left Sigrid unmoved, but she didn't think it politic to say so to one of his collectors.

Trent smiled at her over his glass of wine. "I hope you don't mind my saying, Lieutenant, how surprised I am to see you in such a different setting."

She sketched a half salute with her own glass. "I might say the same, Mr. Trent. I shouldn't have thought you'd be away from your home the first night after your grandson returned. Or didn't he arrive?"

Trent glanced around to see if anyone else was within earshot, then joined Sigrid at the railing with his voice lowered.

"He arrived right on schedule, but I was on the benefit's board of organizers and there might have been questions if I hadn't put in an appearance."

"Did he remember you or your daughter?"

"He doesn't seem to. He was so young when that woman took him. But Sarah knew immediately it was really Jamie. He's still very shy, of course, and she hasn't been able to get him to open up to her; but she's a natural mother and it's just a matter of time."

Sigrid heard confidence in his voice and said, "I'm glad it's turning out well."

Trent smiled into her dark eyes. "You really mean that, don't you?"

"Yes."

"Do you have children, Lieutenant?"

Sigrid shook her head. "One doesn't have to live with pain to visualize it, Mr. Trent."

"No," he said slowly. He leaned against the ship rail, his hands cupped around the plastic wine goblet, and gazed across the river. "No, but there's a special bond between child and parent that has to be experienced to fully appreciate. You seem a perceptive young woman, but I doubt if you can understand the hell my daughter has gone through these past four years. And me. I've had to watch the most important person in my life grieve until her mind almost eroded and know I was helpless to do one damn thing about it!

"When Jamie died—when we thought he was dead, kidnapped and perhaps killed—it was as if Sarah's life and mine had dead-ended. Everything I'd worked for turned to ashes overnight. Children connect you to the world, you know, and to the future. The Old Testament writers were onto something basic and primeval when they wrote about bloodlines and the fruit of one's loins."

"But surely Mrs. Logan is still young, less than thirty?"

"Jamie was the first of her pregnancies to go full term," Trent said flatly. "And even that was dicey. The doctors didn't rule out another child altogether, but they weren't optimistic.

"And frankly, Lieutenant, between Jim Logan's death and Jamie's disappearance, the question of another husband, another baby, was academic. Sarah became suicidal."

Sigrid recalled that Nancy Kuipers had mentioned that Sarah Logan had had a mental breakdown, but she didn't know it had gone that far.

Justin Trent took a deep breath and finished his wine. "All in the past now," he said briskly. "Or will be as soon as all the media hoopla is behind us. If Sarah feels up to it, we'll be announcing Jamie's return tomorrow or the next day. Get it over with."

Remembering the reporters, television cameras and photographers that had swarmed around the Trent house four years ago, Sigrid gave an involuntary shiver.

"I know," Trent said ruefully. "With a little luck, the next time Jamie makes the news will be an obscure little paragraph in *The Wall Street Journal* when he comes into business with me."

He reached for Sigrid's empty glass. "May I get you more wine before I leave?"

"No, thank you."

"Then I'll say good night," he said with a half bow. "That applause we just heard must mean that the formalities are over, the ball has been declared an official success and now I'm free to go home."

"And miss the midnight buffet?" asked Nauman, suddenly reappearing. "How do you get to pass up overcooked crab claws and we don't?"

"Please," Trent smiled with a mock shudder. "I was *not* on the menu committee."

"Good man," said Nauman, watching Trent's erect figure recede down the deck. "Where did you meet him?"

Trusting his discretion, Sigrid told him of Gladwell's murder and described Jamie Logan's return.

"Sounds almost like a Saturday afternoon cliff-hanger," said Nauman, who was old enough to remember them well. "Kidnapped by a drug addict to replace a dead baby, hauled around from one crash pad to another, orphaned and then entrusted to a nutty aunt. And now back into the arms of Midas."

"Trent *is* a Midas, isn't he?"

"I suppose," said Nauman, who was his agent's despair because of his indifference to amassing a fortune. "At any rate, he's bought five of my pictures and never haggled over the price my gallery set. Odd though. Guess that's why he agreed to come tonight."

Sigrid looked at him inquiringly. Usually she could follow when Nauman's train of thought branched off, but she didn't think his "odd" referred to money and said so.

"No, it's just that while I was waiting in there for them to call my name, someone mentioned that tonight's the first time Trent's been on any sort of boat or ship since the kidnapping. They said he gave away that speedboat and had refused to get out on the water ever since."

"You can hardly call a ship moored to a pier 'out on the water,'" Sigrid objected.

"Not me. Trent. According to gossip. Dance?"

"Not to that," she said, hearing a pounding rock beat that vibrated the ballroom.

"I was told there's a jazz quartet playing mellow blues on A Deck." He offered her his arm. "Shall we go see?"

CHAPTER XVIII

Curled up on the couch, her bare feet tucked comfortably beneath her, Sigrid sipped morning coffee and reread for the third time the opening paragraphs of an arms control article in the magazine section of the Sunday *Times*. She couldn't seem to keep her mind on the world's serious problems. Probably the red fingernail polish, she thought, admiring the novelty of painted nails against the newsprint.

In a nearby chair, equally comfortable in brown silk pajamas and tan robe, Roman Tramegra plowed steadily through the front section of the *Times*. Since he always read the Sunday paper in the same order, from back to front, Sigrid guessed he'd been up for two or three hours.

She sneaked a look at the puzzle page and was pleased to see a Double-Crostic this week. Even better, a quick perusal of the clues showed that at least two thirds of them would have to be puzzled over. She disliked it when the definitions were too easy; a good Double-Crostic should take at least forty-five minutes to complete.

Feeling a bit like someone having dessert before finishing the broccoli, Sigrid happily abandoned nuclear disarmament and began trying different letters in the grid to discover if a seventeen-letter "Concord Transcendentalist" meant Henry David Thoreau or Ralph Waldo Emerson.

With its high ceilings and tall windows, the white Victorian house at the edge of the village was cool and pleasant despite a morning sun that was already shimmering the sidewalks outside with thermal waves. Ellen Luft heard the newspaper rustle across the table as her son finished the sports section and lifted her head from her own breakfast. "More milk, Peter?"

"No thanks, Mom."

The red-haired youth looked at his lovely, unworldly mother with something close to despair. The Naughton women had always kept themselves isolated from the rest of the village, and while this had worked to their benefit in some ways, in others it had given them a false sense of security, and he couldn't seem to get through to his mother and aunts an appreciation of their present danger. He sighed and tried again.

"Mom?"

Ellen smiled at the sigh. "Poor old Peter! All the weight of the world on your shoulders. You mustn't worry so, darling. Clayton Gladwell was murdered by someone down in New York. Depend upon it. The police will only be interested in that. No one will care a fig about some old women living way up here in Dowling."

"But if you could just make Aunt Nick think before she blurts things out!"

"I try, Peter. You know I do. But Nicky—of the three sisters, Penny might have had the reputation for smart-mouthing, but Nicky was always the outspoken one."

"And Grandma Dolly the go-along-with-anything one," the boy said bitterly.

"Now, Peter," said his mother, half in warning, half in jest, "you mustn't speak meanly of the dead."

"Dead? Who's dead?" asked Nichole Naughton from the other end of the breakfast table. She turned her ancient beaked head to her niece and grandnephew and strained to hear. "Did someone else die?"

*   *   *

The definition read "Microscopic water wheels? (Phylum Aschelminthes)." There were eight numbered blanks and she already had the last letter, an A. Sigrid thought a moment, then took her ballpoint pen and began writing r-o-t-i-f-e—

"I don't believe it! I do *not* believe it!" howled Roman, flapping the newspaper wildly. "The *idiots*! Those Viennese numbskulls! Whipped cream where their brains should be! And where were the building inspectors? Aren't they supposed to issue permits first?"

"What's happened?" asked Sigrid.

Roman shoved the paper at her. "Look!" he commanded.

Halfway down the page, a four-column photograph showed an ordinary block of nondescript brick buildings in downtown Manhattan. Ordinary except that there was a fresh pile of rubble where the corner building should have been. The story beneath was captioned: *Renovations Cause Building Collapse*.

His deep voice rumbling with disapproval, Roman read aloud, "'As crews finished razing the building and began removing the rubble, the owner of the building told rescuers and firefighters that he had recently removed a wall and several columns to enlarge his pastry shop on the ground floor.'"

"Is that my new apartment?" Sigrid asked in disbelief.

"Was, my dear, *was*," snarled Roman. "I suggest you call your bank first thing tomorrow and stop payment on that deposit check you gave Schnitzler."

He began pawing through the scattered Sunday paper. "Where's the classified section?" he asked wearily.

Sigrid capped her pen and put the puzzle aside. Sunday's peace had fled. Roman would be grumping through rental ads for the next two hours, so she might as well drive over to Queens and look in on Helmut Dussel; see if she could discover what made an invalid septuagenarian a subject for Gladwell's blue folders.

CHAPTER XIX

█

The four adults seated at the table pretended everything was normal, but lunch had become somewhat strained.

"The Mets are playing a home game next Saturday," Justin Trent said in a conversational tone. "Do you like baseball, Jamie?"

Across the table from him, the child nodded mutely.

"Yes, *sir!*" Rachel Elsner corrected sharply.

"Yes, sir," the little boy whispered, glancing fearfully from the woman he had only recently learned to call Aunt to the gray-haired man they said he should now call Grandfather.

"Speak up, boy," said Miss Elsner, pursing her thin lips into a frown.

Sarah Logan looked distressed.

"That's all right," Trent said quickly. "Jamie just has to get used to us again."

"I'm afraid my sister wasn't much on discipline," said Miss Elsner. "Spare the rod and spoil the child."

"You haven't—?" gasped Sarah Logan.

"Whipped him? No, I didn't have to. I'll say this for Mike—I mean, Jamie. He learned right off the bat not to try any tricks with me."

There was an appalled silence hastily filled by a comment from Trent to his other guest.

The boy withdrew his attention from the adults and finished the food on his plate. Since going to live with Aunt Rachel, he'd eaten meals at a table every day, though not as pretty as this one. Aunt Rachel didn't have plates like this or put a cloth on her table.

Mommy's food had tasted better than Aunt Rachel's, but it was good in this new house, too. With Mommy, they'd had doughnuts and Big Macs and pizzas in floppy cartons. Only, that was his other mommy, he remembered. Now there was this nice-smelling lady who smiled at him and kept looking at him all the time and they said she was his real mommy—that the other one had stolen him away because her own little boy had died.

He knew about death. He knew his other mommy had died and not just gone away. ("To heaven I pray, though I very much doubt it," Aunt Rachel had said.) He knew because she had lain there stiff and cold even when he shook her and told her he was hungry. And he'd known she was like the dogs and cats and other small animals they used to find lying stiffly by the road when they were hitching through California.

He sat quietly while the stilted grown-up conversation went on around him.

He would call the man Grandfather and the smiling lady Mother, but he wished they would call him Mike. It was so hard to keep remembering that he was Jamie. His eyelids grew heavy.

Sarah Logan glanced down at the child and said, "Sleepy, Jamie? Shall I take you upstairs to Mary?"

When she allowed herself to believe Jamie was actually coming home, Sarah had tried to hire Nanny back, but that nursemaid had returned to England and could not be coaxed to leave her current position in a baronet's nursery. So Mary Patterson had been found, a cheerful young Scotswoman with a comforting burr in her voice and a sympathetic appreciation of the bewildering circumstances.

The little boy nodded and slipped down from his chair.

"I think he's still affected by the time difference," Sarah told the others.

Rachel Elsner swallowed the last of her dessert and seized her chance to escape.

"Me too," she said, hastily rising. "I think I'll go up for a little Sunday afternoon lay-down myself."

The house and the people who lived there awed her. It was like something out of a movie—gleaming furniture, thick rugs, pictures on the walls, fresh flowers in every room, a color TV in her bedroom, everything kept shiny clean by quiet servants; in fact, push a button and a maid would come, ready to fetch whatever she wanted. And the Trents themselves—Mr. Trent and Mrs. Logan—both so polite and kind, asking how she'd slept and if her room was comfortable and it really wasn't their fault that she felt so out of place even though she knew she was just as good as them in the eyes of the Lord.

When Sarah Logan returned from helping Mary settle Jamie for a nap, the two men had moved into her father's study.

"How much longer does that awful woman have to stay here?" she asked them.

"That depends a bit on you, Sarah," Trent reminded her.

The slender, fair-haired woman smoothed her skirt nervously and took the vacant leather chair next to Trent's desk. "I don't see why *I* have to talk to reporters," she told the other man, who had spoken little during lunch. "Can't you handle everything, Frank?"

"I can do most of it, Mrs. Logan, but not all."

A mild-spoken man of quiet demeanor, Frank Aldrich was senior member of the Trent organization's public relations department. It was his job to keep the Trent name out of the news media except when carefully fostering a favorable corporate image. For four years his staff had helped Trent shield Sara Logan from the uncomfortable glare of flashbulbs, paparazzi, and sob sister interviews and it would do so again; "but right now, I'm afraid you'll have to meet with the press personally," he told her.

"I can give them all the background information about how Jamie was taken and when he was found, but if you don't let their cameras record your in-the-flesh reaction to having your son restored, they're going to hound you till you do. You and Jamie are a news junkie's dream— get it all over with at once is my advice. Let them ask all the questions they can think of in one full-coverage conference, then maybe slip away to Westchester with Jamie while they talk it to death and gear up for the next seven-day wonder."

She smiled. "It sounds so easy when you say it."

"It *is* easy," Trent promised. "Frank and I'll be there to help. We'll bring Jamie out for a few pictures at the end and then it'll be all over."

"Shall I set it up for tomorrow?" asked Aldrich.

"Tomorrow?" Sarah faltered.

"Tomorrow," her father said firmly.

"Just down this hall, Lieutenant," said William Burchlow, trying to match his short stride to the tall woman's long steps.

When two days had passed with no one coming to question him about Clayton Gladwell, the nursing home director had almost decided that they were home free. Now, on their busiest day of the week, here came a police officer nattering about questioning old Helmut.

"I really do think this is unnecessary," he told Lieutenant Harald again. "Poor Mr. Dussel barely remembers his own name. You can't expect him to remember a lawyer he saw only briefly several years ago. *I* handle everything for him. If you have questions about his affairs, ask *me*."

"Oh, I intend to," the flint-eyed woman promised. Nothing in her voice implied a threat, yet Mr. Burchlow suddenly felt apprehensive. There was no way she could know, he told himself. No way in the world. Gladwell had no reason to keep any evidence of their dealings. As long as he kept his head, exercised prudence and tact, everything would continue to operate smoothly.

Other visitors moved through the hall—dutiful relatives; equally ancient friends maintaining a fierce, smug independence; church visitation groups. Most of the rooms they passed had their doors open, and most con-

tained at least two elderly men or women in various
stages of mobility. Some took a turn along the hall with
their visitors, walking with canes or lightweight aluminum walkers. Some were surprisingly agile in wheel-
chairs, others were completely bedridden. Many of them
took no notice of who passed their doors, but several
brightened as Burchlow approached with Sigrid Harald.
One old woman standing by the doorway held out a hand
to Sigrid. "Janice?" she asked.

"No, Mrs. Ambrose, your daughter hasn't come yet,"
Burchlow told her with kindly optimism. "Maybe later."

The old woman's face fell.

As they moved away Burchlow confided, "Sundays get
them restless. Big visiting day, you know, and when their
people don't come, they get depressed. Mrs. Ambrose's
daughter lives three stops away on the subway. You'd
think she'd be here twice a week, right? Not since Christmas, Lieutenant, not since Christmas. In a way, it's easier on men like Mr. Dussel. If they know they have no
family left to visit them, then they don't get as down in
the dumps when nobody comes."

They entered a boxy, utilitarian room—clean enough,
but uninspiring. Two hospital beds were separated by a
narrow aisle and a double dresser. Except for a few
framed photographs hanging on the walls, most personal
effects had been tidied away, no longer needed. The
brightest object in the room was an expensive color television mounted on a bracket over the door. Helmut Dussel, very thin, his skin the hue of tallow wax, held the
remote control in gnarled fingers.

"Well, Mr. Dussel, how are you feeling today?" Burchlow asked heartily.

The old man's eyes flicked from Burchlow to Sigrid
and back to the television where a ball game was in
progress.

"Why don't we turn down the television so we can
talk?" asked Burchlow, and tried to take the remote control.

Dussel's fingers tightened around it stubbornly.

The wizened old man in the next bed had been dozing

but he came awake now, his eyes bright and curious as Sigrid approached his roommate's bedside.

"Mr. Dussel, I'm a police officer. May I ask you a few questions about Clayton Gladwell?"

For an answer, Dussel frowned and clicked the channel selector. Ball games all over the nation flashed across the overhead screen, interspersed with old movies, talking heads, and a track meet.

"*Stoppen Sie* there!" cried the occupant of the other bed and Dussel obediently ceased switching channels and began to watch young athletes race around the broad ovals.

"He don't speak much English," explained the second man in a heavy Italian accent.

"Do you speak German, then?" asked Sigrid.

"Not really—just a few words I picked up here and there from him. Enough so we get along."

"Not too much talking, Mr. Scocozza," warned Burchlow. "Heart condition," he told Sigrid.

"That's it," agreed Mr. Scocozza cheerfully, and now Sigrid noticed the paleness of his lips and how he seemed to breathe with a bit of difficulty.

"Have you and Mr. Dussel been roommates long?"

"Seven years," answered Mr. Burchlow impatiently. "Really, Lieutenant, I can answer—"

There was a crash down the hallway, the clatter of a metal tray loaded with glassware hitting the floor. Burchlow rushed from the room to see what had happened.

"Hey, missus, how come everybody's so interested in old Dussel?" asked Scocozza.

"Everybody? Has someone else been here recently? Mr. Burchlow said he hadn't had visitors in years."

"That's what I mean. Nobody, then that guy a couple of days ago and now you. He tried to ask Dussel about the same guy, too."

"Clayton Gladwell?"

"Sounded like that. He was a little short fat guy."

"Did Mr. Dussel talk to him?"

"Naw. I'm telling you—he can't speak much English and he don't like to try no more. Later we were jawing back and forth in Dutch language and I ask him, 'Who was Gladwell?' and he just shrugs like he never heard the name. So who is he, missus?"

The invalid's bright eyes were so eager, Sigrid couldn't refuse.

"He was a lawyer who once handled an inheritance for Mr. Dussel."

"Inheritance? Oh, yeah, I remember. An uncle of Dussel's back in the old country. Left him enough to stay here. Me, I gotta sell everything my Tina and me work for and turn over my Social Security too."

"Did Mr. Gladwell ever visit here?"

"Never," said Scocozza. "Nobody." His eyes became even brighter with unexpected tears. "Who's to come? Dussel never had a family here and me, who's gonna come see me with my boy dead in Korea and my Tina buried the same year?"

His head sank deeper into the pillows and his eyes closed, but tears brimmed past the shut lids to slip down the wrinkled cheeks unheeded.

On the television over her head, an excited announcer babbled of world records while a young pole vaulter launched himself into the air. Blue skies framed the slim lithe body as it arced over the white bar and somersaulted through Texas sunlight.

Helmut Dussel watched impassively.

Sigrid breathed an inward sigh and stepped out into the hallway to find Burchlow near the end of a confrontation with one of his white-uniformed workers. Anger blotched the aide's plump cheeks and her brown eyes crackled with hostility.

"You don't talk to me like that!" she shrilled, dropping the pieces of glass she'd begun to pick up when Burchlow rushed out to blame her. "You fire me? Then clean it up yourself, Mister Big Shot. I quit!"

She whirled from the scene of the accident, abandoned her cart loaded with trays of filled juice glasses and stalked away from Burchlow's expostulations.

At the sight of the tall policewoman's inquiring face among the others who had gathered, the director gave himself a mental shake and told the onlookers, "Nothing to worry about, friends. Accidents happen. We'll have this cleaned up in no time. Be careful going by, Mrs. Jamison. We don't want you slipping on any juice and breaking that other hip."

The curious dispersed, their bit of excitement over, and Burchlow went to a nearby house phone. When the main desk answered he said, "Rosa? A tray of juice has been spilled up here. Send Higgins to mop it up. And, Rosa? Ms. Quentzl has quit. See that she cleans out her locker and turns in her keys before she leaves; then tell Sally to finish serving juice on this floor when she's through on the first. We'll have to double up for a couple of days."

He turned back to Sigrid with an unruffled smile. "Incompetent help. The bane of every organization, Lieutenant, as I'm sure you must know. Did you finish with Mr. Dussel?"

"For now."

"Excellent. If you don't mind finding your own way out, I'd better wait here until the orderly comes."

Sigrid turned a cold eye on the director's hopeful face. "You forget that we were going to discuss Mr. Dussel's affairs downstairs," she said. "Or would you prefer to bring his papers to my office tomorrow?"

"No, no, now will be fine," said Burchlow.

On the stairs they met a man in rumpled hospital whites, carrying mop and pail, a sullen look on his ugly face. There was something about the man's pugilistic build that made Sigrid look at him twice. He glared back, but kept walking.

"Has that man worked for you long?" she asked.

"Higgins? About a month now, why?"

"He reminds me of someone I've seen somewhere," she said. It occurred to her that the somewhere was probably in a lineup or night court or someplace similar that Burchlow might not approve of. More than one ex-con found it easier to get work if they were reticent about their past. Far be it from her to queer a man's attempt at honest work.

She followed Burchlow into his office past the smiling young receptionist, who was told to call the employment agency next morning to arrange for Ms. Quentzl's replacement.

Soon Sigrid was looking through Helmut Dussel's records. Born in Austria, he had come to the United States shortly after World War II, taken out citizenship papers, and conducted a modest beer and wine import business. With no family to take over, the business had been sold upon his retirement. He had entered Lantana Walk almost eight years ago after a minor stroke, coupled with degenerative arthritis, had left him unable to continue living alone.

"The hospital took most of his savings," said Burchlow, "and he was nearly down to Social Security when Mr. Gladwell located him."

The attorney had come out to verify Dussel's identity for the West German trustees, but the old man had been confused by all the technicalities, "so Mr. Gladwell drew up a power of attorney to let me act for him and Mr. Dussel signed it."

The inheritance consisted of interest on a trust still held in West Germany. Upon Helmut Dussel's death it would revert to distant cousins in Austria, but until then quarterly payments were channeled to Dussel's bank account in Queens.

"The money is used to meet his monthly expenses here and whatever else he wants of a personal nature—clothes, cigarettes, the television, et cetera."

Sigrid thought there hadn't been too much et cetera in that bare room Dussel and Scocozza shared upstairs.

"How much income is it exactly?" she asked and held out her hand for the bank statement.

Unexpectedly, Burchlow dug in his heels. "No, I'm sorry, Lieutenant. These are personal financial records of a poor old man who has a right to privacy. You saw him. It's ridiculous to think he could have known anything about Mr. Gladwell's murder. Mr. Gladwell hasn't been here in over five years."

"Then why has Mr. Dussel paid him two hundred dollars a month all these years?"

William Burchlow looked shocked that she knew.

"He—he handled legal matters for Mr. Dussel," he stammered.

Sigrid continued to gaze at him coolly.

"It was a like a finder's fee," said Burchlow, fumbling with his gold cuff links. "A percentage of that inheritance that he and Gladwell agreed on right at the beginning."

"In cash?"

"That was the way he—that was their agreement: two hundred-dollar bills in an envelope mailed to his home address every month. As Mr. Dussel's agent, I have continued to carry out his wishes."

"If that's all those bank statements will show, then why make me go through the legalities of a subpoena to see them?" asked Sigrid, well aware that she was on shaky ground in that area.

Burchlow started to answer, thought better of it, and gave a small shrug that didn't come off quite as unconcernedly as he hoped. "I'm sorry, Lieutenant. Ethically, my hands are tied."

"Then let me ask you this, Mr. Burchlow: Where were you last Thursday between five and six P.M.?"

"*Me?* You think *I*—? Oh, now, wait just a minute!" he squeaked, pushing his chair back from his desk until it banged the wall behind in his instinctive anxiety to put as much physical distance as possible between the police and himself.

"I was right here. A hundred people must have seen me!"

From his chair against the wall, Burchlow struggled for composure. "That's it. I'm sorry. No more questions. You want to talk to me or Mr. Dussel, then you get that subpoena and I'll get my lawyer."

To his infinite relief she stood up, thanked him for his time and showed herself out of his office.

He would have been rattled all over again if he could have overheard her telephone conversation with Detective Elaine Albee a few minutes later.

CHAPTER XX

Weather forecasters were promising some sort of relief by the middle of the week, but on Monday morning the heat wave still dominated. The air hanging over the city was thick with diesel fumes, brackish river smells and what a local stand-up comic called *eau de landfill*.

Sigrid was glad to enter headquarters' air-conditioned coolness. She was on time, yet Tillie was there before her, already immersed in autopsy and ballistics reports on the bullet that had killed Clayton Gladwell.

"Nothing unusual about it," he told Sigrid. "Just an ordinary .22 rimfire. Distinctive markings, though. Ought to be an easy match when we find the gun. I'm running a check on all the names in the case to see if any of them were ever issued permits for a .22."

"It wasn't Trent's, then?" she asked, referring to the Smith & Wesson pistol the financier had given her Friday evening.

"Nope. They say it hasn't been recently fired and the markings weren't even close." He looked at her curiously. "Did you think Trent was our killer?"

Sigrid shrugged. "At this point, almost anyone could be."

"I don't know, Lieutenant. Trent's movements check out according to Lowry, and Nancy Kuipers and Jean

Parrish seem to have been where they said. Even the Bhattacherjeas' alibis check. By the way, there was a message from Albee to tell you she got the job and starts this afternoon. Is that something to do with this case?"

"I hope so," Sigrid said, and gave him a full account of her visit to the Lantana Walk Nursing Home the previous afternoon, of Burchlow's reluctance to show Dussel's financial records or to discuss his dealings with Gladwell, and of the aide who had resigned in anger. "I thought it wouldn't hurt to let one of our people apply for the opening, poke around for a day or so."

Tillie looked up from the notes he'd made as she talked and said, "The short fat guy that tried to see Dussel on Friday—Dan Embry?"

"Sounds like him, Tillie, but why should he suddenly turn up there?"

"Maybe for the same reason Gladwell had a blue folder on Dussel?" Tillie wrote himself a reminder to speak to Embry again. "And I've arranged for someone to be at Global Airlines when Miss Barr's pilot comes in this evening."

Sigrid opened the fat manila envelope on her desk and Tillie made a pleased sound when he saw that it held Xeroxes of the lab's reconstruction of the charred scraps of paper found in Gladwell's wastebasket Thursday night.

Their pleasure soon turned to disappointment, though, for there seemed little to help them. The bits of photographs were publicity stills of Elena Dorato. A few salvaged lines of newsprint detailed someone's appearance of malnutrition and probably had some relevance to a partial headline—"Elderly Rouse Fears of Abuse"—but rang no bells for Tillie or Sigrid. There were scraps of some legal documents—one seemed to be a contract, the other a will, but all identifying passages had been burned beyond recovery. Enough had been saved of one item to show that it had been a pro forma letter from Justin Trent appointing Clayton Gladwell his agent to make inquiries into the whereabouts of his grandson, James Trent Logan. Finally there was the top half of a Putnam County death certificate issued for

Dolinda Naughton McIntosh about two and a half years earlier.

The rest of the burned paper had been carbonized scraps impossible for the lab to reconstruct.

"Detective Tildon?"

They glanced up.

The young man who stood in the doorway looked as if he'd just stepped from some ivy league campus to which he'd be returning as soon as summer classes began. He was of medium height, square-jawed, and his blond hair was cut short and combed back in a neat wave. He wore chinos and a navy blue knit shirt with a tiny animal appliqued on the breast pocket, and his gleaming teeth displayed a smile that never quite erased a certain vacancy in his blue eyes.

"I'm Tildon," Tillie said.

"They told me you wanted to see me," said the newcomer with another easy display of those perfect teeth. "I'm Bailey Dunne."

Tillie looked at Sigrid blankly.

"Clayton Gladwell's private investigator."

"Of course. Come in, Mr. Dunne."

He was given a chair and invited to share both their coffee and an account of his dealings with the murdered lawyer.

"Sure," he said to both. "Three sugars, no cream, please. And I'm always glad to cooperate with the police, but I don't see how I can be much help. I'd only known Gladwell a couple of months. I guess they told you about my arrangements with him?"

"We'd prefer to hear it from you," said Sigrid.

Very well, Dunne told them. He had joined the Navy immediately upon graduating from high school and had spent his first hitch with the Shore Patrol and his second with Naval Intelligence.

"The Navy was okay, but I figured I wasn't going anywhere in peacetime without a college degree and OCS. Civilian life's where the money is and a P.I. doesn't need a baccalaureate—just chutzpah and a little luck."

Again the smile.

"I've kept busy enough this past year, but nothing big,

and with office rents what they are in this town, I was really lucky to meet up with Gladwell. He gave me a place to hang my hat, a telephone number for the yellow pages, and part-time use of a cute little English typist. All I had to do was give him first priority on my time. Not bad."

"Did he give you much work?"

"Nope, not really. Not unless you count finding little Jamie Logan."

He said it smugly, as if he thought it would be a bombshell. He was deflated when the two police detectives indicated they'd already heard his astounding news.

"Exactly how did you locate the boy?" asked Sigrid.

Sulkily, Dunne admitted that he'd only used leads his predecessor had uncovered.

"But I was the one who followed her trail to California, and I was the one who buttered a few hands at welfare and AFDC offices in Sacramento—that's Aid to Families with Dependent Children," he elucidated.

"We know," she told him gently.

"I turned up three E. Elsners. After that, it was just a process of elimination to pick up on *my* E. Elsner down in Laguna Beach. Except that she'd o.d.'d and the kid had been given to the aunt in L.A. Lucky for me, the Laguna Beach police had her address.

"She was happy as a clam when I turned up last week about the boy. She didn't want her sister's leavings. Gladwell wouldn't let me tell her who the kid might be, of course; not that it mattered. She quit being nosy as soon as I slipped her a couple of hundred. We trotted right along to a doctor and got the kid's blood typed. Perfect match." He smoothed his blond wave modestly as if personally responsible for the child's blood type.

"Odd that Gladwell would change investigators when he was so close," Sigrid mused aloud. "Why do you suppose he did, Mr. Dunne?"

"Probably because he didn't know how close old Dave was," he said breezily.

"Dave?"

"Dave Shovener. He was the one who recommended me to Gladwell. Said he and Gladwell couldn't get along.

Said Gladwell made him eat dirt and big case or not, he wasn't going to take it any longer. But then, after Gladwell gave me the job, Dave was a real sport about it—gave me everything he had. Hell, he was even the one who suggested checking out the AFDC office. I'd have thought about it sooner or later, of course, but he made it sooner. Guess I should have gone there first instead of messing around with the Department of Motor Vehicles. It would have saved me a month."

"Where can we find this Dave Shovener?" asked Tillie.

Bailey Dunne looked uncomfortable.

"That's just it. He went to Chicago and sort of dropped out of sight. I was out there this week, thought I'd look him up, tell him how the case turned out before it hit the papers. I asked around and they told me old Dave got himself killed. He must have walked in on somebody ripping off his apartment because he would up taking two through the chest. First Dave and now Gladwell. Hell of a note, isn't it?" he asked sententiously.

They agreed that it was.

Sigrid handed him a list of names they'd taken from Gladwell's blue folders:

> Helmut Dussel
> William Burchlow
> Dr. Moraji Bhattacherjea
> Dr. Ishrad Bhattacherjea
> Penelope Naughton
> Elena Dorato
> Howard Tachs

"Did you ever run across any of these people in connection with your work for Gladwell?"

Dunne shook his head. "Nope. Wait a minute! These doctors—the Batterjees or however you pronounce it. That was the first thing I did for Gladwell. Something about getting the niece's visa changed. Gladwell asked me to pick up her records from the local public school in Brooklyn Heights, but she wasn't enrolled there. I told Gladwell and he said he must have made a mistake about the address and anyhow, it wasn't important."

"What school?" asked Tillie.

"Gee, I forget the number. It was the one on Dawson Avenue."

Further questioning elicited no more information. Dunne's mild blue eyes opened even wider at the suggestion that Gladwell had run a blackmail operation on the side, and Sigrid was beginning to feel that she'd lived through this conversation before.

They took the names of two Chicago policemen, former members of Naval Intelligence, with whom Dunne said he'd been having a drink at the time Gladwell was killed, and then let him go.

"Why does Bailey Dunne remind me of Jean Parrish?" Sigrid asked Tillie.

"Same amount of smarts?" he suggested. "Same lack of curiosity about Gladwell's motives?"

"Probably. What was that about the school? Your ears were almost quivering."

She seldom bantered with him and Tillie beamed at her light tone. "Nothing really," he said. "Only that's the same school Bhattacherjea told me the kid was attending. Should I send somebody to find out who's told the truth?"

"Fine. And while you're at it, I'll talk to Chicago and see what they know about Dave Shovener."

As Tillie gathered up all his notes and papers, Sigrid leaned back in her chair and pulled out a road map from the bookcase behind her. "Feel like a drive?" she asked him.

CHAPTER XXI

▐

Two counties upriver from the city, the July afternoon felt several degrees cooler. Green lawns and leafy oaks made summer pleasurable there. Far from the city's airless streets and the push and shove of too many people, several comfortable old-fashioned wicker chairs with faded chintz cushions were grouped on a wide stone terrace overlooking the Hudson River in the distance. Here in Putnam County there were stretches of the river still heavily wooded along the banks and still relatively untouched.

In one of the wicker chairs, an old man sat drowsing in dappled sunlight.

"Just go on out," the pleasant-faced housekeeper had told them. "He loves company."

Sigrid and Tillie stood for a moment enjoying the view, reluctant to disturb the doctor's siesta. From this height the village of Dowling-on-Hudson presented only a few rooftops and a couple of church steeples through the dense trees below.

"Dr. Freeman?" said Tillie.

The old man opened his eyes and gave them a friendly smile.

"How nice to see you." He pulled himself erect and

straightened his glasses. "Do sit down. Did Mrs. Smith give you something to drink?"

He was tall and rather fragile-looking, with thin white hair and bushy eyebrows, but his eyes were alert as he peered at Tillie through glasses which had promptly slid back down his nose. "You're one of Albert Rush's boys, aren't you?"

"No, sir, we're from New York," Tillie said. "Police. I'm Detective Tildon and this is Lieutenant Harald."

"Police? Oh, dear," he smiled, pushing up his glasses. "Have I done something wrong?"

"We're here because of a death certificate you signed three years ago," Sigrid said.

"Three years? That can't be right. I've been retired—let's see now, I took in my shingle when I was seventy-five and I'm what now? Eighty-three? Eighty-four? You must be mistaken."

"We called the county clerk's office over in Carmel," said Tillie. "They said Dr. Asa Freeman of Dowling-on-Hudson."

"That's me," he agreed.

"It was for Mrs. Dolinda Naughton McIntosh."

"Oh. Dolly. Yes, of course."

"Can you tell us about it?"

Dr. Freeman turned in his chair. "Where's Mrs. Smith? She makes wonderful lemonade. Just the ticket on a hot day like this."

As if she'd read his mind, the housekeeper emerged from the terrace door with a large pitcher of iced lemonade and three glasses.

It was as wonderful as Dr. Freeman had promised, tart and cold with slices of lemons floating among the ice cubes. Delicious, but Sigrid thought she recognized delaying tactics as the doctor distributed and refilled glasses ("The first for thirst, a refill for taste," he said), made them pull their chairs into deeper shade, and talked of the heat wave.

Approaching from another angle, Sigrid said, "I suppose in a small town like Dowling, the Naughton family must have been longtime friends as well as patients."

"Why, yes," he agreed cautiously. "I can even remember old Jefferson Naughton, the girls' grandfather. He was the one who started the shoe factory back in 1864."

"Shoes?"

"Used to be the biggest business in town. Naughton Shoes. 'There's Naught like Naughton's.' That was their motto. Went under during the Depression."

"That must have been a disappointment to the family."

"It was. It was. Especially to Penny. Nick and Dolly— the other two sisters, Nichole and Dolinda—didn't blame her for it. Factories all over the country were going bust. But she was so sure she could hang on to it. See, their father, Jeff Naughton's only boy, had the brains of a butterfly. Thought the factory was like a gold mine. Something you took money out of and never put a cent back in.

"When he died, he left the management to Penny. Thought 'cause she was such hot stuff down in New York that she'd got her grandfather's business sense. Hell, Penny was bright, but she didn't know any more about running a shoe factory than you do. 'Specially one that'd been let go down.

"She sent up some fancy Dan from the city to manage it. They bought new equipment, retooled the line to make high-fashion ladies' shoes and never even noticed that the country was too broke to buy dancing shoes. Good solid brogans, that's what was needed. A couple of factories on up the river made millions during the war. Army boots and suchlike. And there was Penny, trying to keep the world in patent-leather slippers. Took almost every dime they had. She felt the disgrace very keenly when the bank foreclosed."

"Is that why she left New York?" asked Sigrid.

"Have some more lemonade," said Dr. Freeman, and filled their glasses again with a surprisingly steady hand.

"We mustn't impose on your hospitality," said Sigrid. "If you could just tell us how you happened to sign Mrs. McIntosh's death certificate so long after your retirement?"

"I still saw one or two of my longtime patients. Like

the Naughton girls. They didn't hold with any of the young doctors in town then. 'I'm not stripping for somebody young enough to be my grandson,' Penny said. Didn't matter. All three of 'em healthy as horses.

"Then Penny called one day. Said Dolly was feeling strange. I went down to see. Looked her over, took her blood pressure. It was a little high. Nothing to worry about, but she said she knew she was going to die. I told her it was a lot of nonsense, but damned if she didn't.

"Three days later. Her heart just quit working," he said.

"And in your mind, there was nothing unusual about her death?"

The doctor pushed his glasses back up on his nose and glared at Sigrid. "The woman died of heart failure. Happens every day. Nothing unusual about that. She was a strong-minded woman. Said she was going to die and did."

"Very well, Dr. Freeman. We appreciate your talking to us."

Sigrid set her glass back on the tray and started to rise, but Dr. Freeman put out a restraining hand.

"You two aren't going to go bothering the Naughtons, are you?"

"I'm afraid they're involved in a homicide investigation."

"Down in New York? Ridiculous! They haven't left Dowling in years. Anyhow, haven't they had enough troubles without having to answer a lot of tomfool questions?"

Tillie said, "What sort of troubles, sir?"

He spoke in such sympathetic tones that the doctor turned to him as to a potential ally who would help shelter his old friends.

"Nothing but grief the last forty years," he said. "First the factory, then Dolly's husband killed in the war. Penny made Dolly bring her little girl back here to Dowling; gave them a home, and helped Dolly raise her. Ellen. What a pretty child she was! Same red hair as all the Naughtons and a keen mind. More like Penny than

Dolly, only without Penny's vinegar on her tongue. Everybody loved Ellen. Especially Penny.

"And Bill Luft too. Sweethearts since kindergarten. She wanted to be a pediatrician like Bill, open a clinic here in Dowling. They'd just finished their last year of pre-med. Penny drove over to Connecticut to bring them home for the summer and her car skidded off the highway, went up in flames. She and the baby—young Peter—were in the back seat and they were thrown clear. By the time they got Ellen out, her sight was gone. Bill didn't make it at all."

Dr. Freeman's glasses had slid down to the very end of his nose again, but he seemed not to notice. His thoughts were turned inward, remembering that time of grief.

"Penny went wild. Spent the rest of her money taking Ellen to every eye specialist in the country. In the end, she had to accept what I'd first told her. Ellen's blindness was permanent.

"They had to scrimp and save and stretch every dollar twice and it was like gall to Penny. She blamed herself for losing the factory, and she blamed herself for the accident even though Bill had been driving."

"But her books have always sold," said Sigrid. "Didn't she have royalties coming in?"

"Everything was tied up," said Dr. Freeman. "A lifetime annuity. Penny explained it to me once. Back in the thirties, her agent got worried because she was pouring so much money into the business up here. He was afraid she was going to wind up without a cent in her old age, so he talked her into putting all her royalties into an annuity. Got a lawyer and two bankers to set one up so tight there'd be no way she could ever break it. Figured that even if she lost the business, she'd still have enough to live on every month.

"Good thing he did, 'cause she'd have spent it all trying to get Ellen's sight back. Good man, that agent. Often wish I could have shaken his hand. He must have loved her, too."

Quietly, Tillie asked, "Were you ever married, Doctor?"

"Couldn't have the one I wanted," he said gruffly. "Didn't want the ones I could have."

"At least they can't have many money worries now," said Sigrid.

"How's that?"

"We understood that a movie company's bought the film rights to the Naughty Penny biography," she said.

"More aggravation than it's worth," he told them. "Poking around in people's lives."

"Especially now that she's bedridden?" asked Tillie.

"Who?"

"Miss Naughton. We heard she was an invalid."

"Nick? What's wrong with her?" He looked bewildered. "They didn't tell me."

"Not Nichole Naughton," said Tillie. "Penelope."

"Oh. Penny. Yes. They've got a new doctor now. Young Simmons. Forgive a senile old man," he said. "They tell me things and I forget them. More lemonade? The ice has almost melted, but Mrs. Smith will bring more."

They declined with thanks, apologized for interrupting his afternoon rest and left.

As they walked around the house to the car, past sweet-smelling roses and mock oranges, Sigrid reflected that self-proclaimed senility made a convenient excuse to change the subject and wander far afield.

As a kid growing up in the Bronx, Detective Peters equated summer with no school, so he didn't actually expect to find anyone at the Dawson Avenue school in the middle of July. However, he'd had to go to Borough Hall to interview some witnesses on another case, and as long as he was in the neighborhood, so to speak, he'd decided to swing past the school.

The doors were all locked, but he heard a typewriter through an open window just above head level, so he went back and pounded on the nearest door.

The typing stopped and a man appeared at the window. "Yes?"

Peters identified himself and asked if he could speak to the principal.

The man withdrew and soon the door was unlocked and Detective Peters found himself face to face with a fiftyish black man, slightly taller than himself, with shrewd dark eyes and salt-and-pepper hair.

"I'm the principal," he said. "Greene."

Peters followed him into an office piled high with neat stacks of student folders.

"My secretary decided to have her baby the last day of school, so I'm behind in my paperwork," he said. "Just put those new spelling books on the floor and have a seat."

Feeling a wave of nostalgia for spelling bees, arithmetic races and recess, Peters drew up the chair and explained that he'd been sent to verify that the Bhattacherjeas' niece, Halima Mutesa, was indeed a student there as they'd been told.

Mr. Greene rose and consulted the file cabinets that lined his office.

"Are you sure you have the right name? I can't find anything under either Mutesa or Bhattacherjea."

"All I know is what they told me," Peters said and again spelled out the names he had.

"Let me check the inactive files," Mr. Greene said finally.

In a few minutes, he returned with an open folder. "Ah, yes. Now I remember. She was only with us a few months. She scored rather high on the nonverbal tests. There was a language problem, of course. Her teacher felt there was something odd about the child's situation and I meant to check into it, but then she was withdrawn from school. Her guardian, Dr. Bhattacherjea, said she was returning to Africa, so I didn't pursue it. Didn't she go? Is she in trouble?"

"I don't know about trouble," said Peters, "but she's still living right here in Brooklyn Heights according to our information."

"And not in school?" frowned Mr. Greene. "No one's asked for her transcript."

He reached for his telephone. "We shall see about that."

• • •

Ellen Luft replaced the telephone receiver with trembling hands, but tried to make her voice calm as she turned back to the two elderly Naughton sisters.

"Darlings," she said, "that was Asa Freeman. Two police officers left his house a little while ago and he thinks they're on their way here."

"Police officers?" cried Nichole Naughton. "Here? Why?"

"They found a copy of that death certificate he signed. Found it in that murdered lawyer's office."

The two old women, both so much alike with their beaked noses and once-red hair, began to exclaim and dither.

"Please stop," said Ellen, her blind face turning from one to the other. "They don't *know* anything. It's probably just their routine, visiting all the man's clients so they can eliminate those who obviously had nothing to do with his death.

"Please, darlings, don't worry. Just help me. You can stay if you wish, Nicky, but Asa says they're expecting Penny to be an invalid. So upstairs and into a bed jacket, darling, and *do* try to look feeble if they insist upon seeing you."

Penny shot from the room while Nick helped Ellen clear away the evidence that three people had eaten a late lunch at that table.

"I shall be deafer than usual," Nick announced magisterially. "That usually puts everyone off. Where is Peter?"

"He had a ball game this afternoon. I hope he doesn't come back till they've been and gone."

She finished loading the tray of dishes and, with the ease of long familiarity with every inch of the old Naughton house, carried it out to the kitchen without jiggles or hesitation. But she banged it down on the counter and said with unwonted vehemence, "I *hate* making him part of this, Nick."

"We've done nothing wrong," her aunt said sternly.

"Then why are we so upset that the police are coming?" asked Ellen wryly.

"You and Peter had nothing to do with it. The only

one who bent the law a little was Asa, and he did it because Penny made him."

"He must have loved her very much when they were young."

"She was a fool not to take him," sniffed Nick. "Just as you're a fool not to take Luke Simmons."

It was an old argument and Ellen smiled without replying. Instead, she began to stack the dishwasher with deft hands. Now that the movie sale had given them money again, they could afford to have a girl from the village come in twice a week for the heavy cleaning, but Ellen continued to perform the routine chores. During the years of scrimping, the needs of those who depended on her had forced her to adjust to her blindness—first Peter as an infant; then later, as they grew older and less able, her mother and two aunts.

Now there were only the two sisters left. Next year Peter would be off to college, and then on his own. Soon, for the first time, there might be time to think of her own needs and wants.

Luke Simmons had a nice voice. People told her his face wasn't exactly handsome, but ruggedly pleasant. Those same people told her she was still beautiful.

She touched her face lightly. There had been almost no scarring from the flames that had taken her sight, but she knew her face must have aged in the sixteen years that had passed since she last saw it in the mirror. What did Dr. Simmons see when he dropped by, ostensibly to examine Nick and Penny?

"Not many doctors make house calls these days," they teased her.

Maybe—just *maybe*—if they got past this afternoon safely, she would tell him that she'd changed her mind; that she *would* go to Peter's next ball game with him.

The doorbell interrupted her musings and, straightening her shoulders with true Naughton valor, she walked down the long hallway like a cheerful Christian martyr off to meet the lions.

Detective Elaine Albee glanced at the clock over the reception desk and wondered if she had enough time for a quick telephone call before she returned to her duties on the second floor.

"Telephone?" said Rosa, who had showed her around the staff lounge. "Here, use this one."

She started to pass the instrument across the counter, but Albee mumbled something about not using an employer's phone for personal business.

"Boyfriend?" grinned the friendly receptionist. "It's your quarter. The pay phone's just around the corner."

"Thanks."

She'd hoped for an old-fashioned booth; unfortunately the telephone was of modern design, with only a plastic hood for privacy. Still, there was nobody near, only a few patients at the end of the hall.

The number she dialed rang several times before a bored voice said, "Dietrich."

"Hi, Dietrich. It's Albee. Is Lieutenant Harald there? Or Tildon?"

"Nope. They left together before lunch. Take a message for you?"

"No, I'll catch them later."

She hung up, disappointed. And yet, what could she have accomplished over the phone? Ask them to run the name Rick Higgins through the computers and see what got kicked out? Probably a phony name; probably have to check the mug files to find him. Find him she would, though. That villainous face was one she'd seen before, even if she couldn't quite remember the context.

She smoothed the skirt of her white uniform over trim hips, gave a friendly salute to Rosa as she passed the desk and hurried up the stairs to her charges on the second floor.

It was time she talked to Mr. Dussel.

CHAPTER XXII

In her extreme age, thought Sigrid, Penelope Naughton seemed to have mellowed at last into a pleasantly conventional old woman.

She wore a green bed jacket and lay propped on several pillows upon an ornate bed of Edwardian vintage. Her hair, cut short to fluff around her face, was almost completely white. Only an echo of pale rust recalled its former flaming glory, and even her nose seemed less beaked.

Her eyes, however, were still intelligent, and her voice barely quavered as she described to Sigrid and Tillie how Clayton Gladwell had entered her life.

"It was about three months after—after my sister died that we had a letter from him. He said he'd heard through confidential sources that a movie company wanted to film my life story, and he would represent my interests if I'd let him. Well, it seemed so providential, didn't it, Ellen? Our own lawyer—dear Theodore Dworkin—died years ago and I really don't think he would have understood film contracts, though of course he was such a *good* man. So honest."

"More honest than Gladwell?" asked Sigrid.

Miss Naughton looked startled. "Did I imply that he was dishonest? I didn't mean to. I merely meant that

136

Theo would not have anticipated all the loopholes that Mr. Gladwell seemed to. He would have expected the other party to deal as honorably as he. Not that the film company wasn't strictly honorable, too. Oh, dear!"

"Lieutenant Harald understands that you aren't trying to slander anyone, darling," Ellen Luft soothed.

"Of course," Sigrid said neutrally.

"So that's all there was to it. Mr. Gladwell came up only twice. Once to discuss the terms with us—the film people wanted to interview me. They actually thought I would give them details of what went on in my bedroom! Of course I told him that was out of the question. I would lend my papers to the project but not my person. The second time he came was to sign contracts. We haven't seen him since."

"The contract you signed gave Gladwell twelve percent of the money you received?" asked Sigrid.

"That was his commission."

"In addition, you've been paying him three hundred dollars a month in cash for the last two years. May we ask why? And why did he have a copy of your sister's death certificate?"

Penny Naughton turned alarmingly pale. "It—was—it—because—Ellen?" she implored.

"Don't get excited, darling. Here, sip this."

Ellen helped her aunt to a glass of juice and patted her thin arm comfortingly as the old woman drank.

"What my aunt is embarrassed to tell you," said Ellen Luft, "is that Gladwell took an extra percentage in cash. It seemed excessive and, well, *unusual* to us; but without his help my aunt would have had nothing, so she didn't quibble. Why he had my mother's death certificate, I couldn't say."

Sigrid began to feel as if multiple layers of fine gauze were being wafted over her. She hadn't really expected to find an unrepentant, wisecracking old tartar who could have hopped down to New York and blasted Gladwell out of her way, but neither had she expected this gentle, easily rattled recluse. If asked, she would have admitted disappointment.

She remembered the bawdy limericks and racy anec-

dotes that Roman Tramegra had told her about the
Naughty Penny of the Roaring Twenties, the famous beds
she'd hopped in and out of, her wicked tongue. Sad to
think that time could have quenched so much fire.

Sigrid didn't doubt for a moment their statement that
Gladwell had visited only twice. With his shrewd eye
for the main chance, he would have been a cat among
the pigeons here. So soon after the other sister's death,
he must have quickly ferreted out whatever mystery
surrounded her sudden demise and held it over them.

Dr. Freeman must be in on the secret, too, coming
out of retirement to certify a death they couldn't slip
past a younger doctor.

The nervousness of these people hung like a palpable
veil between them. Sigrid felt like ripping it aside, yet
what would be gained?

Even if she bullied or tricked their story from them
as Gladwell must have done, it was obvious that neither
Penny nor her niece Ellen nor even that adamantly deaf
Nick downstairs could have sallied into New York alone
and accosted Gladwell without its being noted by a
hundred witnesses.

She might be curious about what had actually happened here two years ago, but Putnam County was outside her jurisdiction. She stood abruptly.

Such visible relief flowed from the two Naughton
women at the signs of her departure that Sigrid couldn't
resist letting them know she wasn't completely taken in.

"We stopped by Dr. Simmons's office briefly before
coming here," she said. "Dr. Freeman told us he was
your family physician now. He was surprised to hear you
weren't feeling well lately, Miss Naughton, and said he'll
drop in to examine you later."

The old woman gasped and sought Ellen's face. The
younger woman touched her arm reassuringly. "I'll be
back in a few minutes, dear, as soon as I've shown our
visitors out."

As Sigrid and Tillie followed Ellen Luft's slender, erect
figure down the broad staircase, Sigrid considered Dr.
Simmons's description of Penelope Naughton's health.

"Bedridden?" he'd said. "Why, no. Just the opposite.

Oh, she couldn't run a marathon," he had smiled boyishly, "but she's able to negotiate the stairs and she still putters in the back flower garden when the weather's nice. Quite remarkable for a woman her age. Both of them are."

If her health was so remarkable, thought Sigrid, why had she sent her sister Nick to New York with their final blackmail payment? Why, too, had she pleaded invalidism when Gladwell first approached her about the movie rights to her story?

And something Dr. Freeman had told them . . .

They continued across the hall to the porch and Sigrid was so engrossed in following that line of speculation that she missed Tillie's puzzled look. He expected her to ask of young Peter Luft's whereabouts last Thursday; and when she didn't, Tillie put the question to Mrs. Luft himself.

Nichole Naughton joined her niece on the wide porch. Now that the police were leaving, her hearing seemed to be sharper.

"There was a ball game," she said. "My nephew plays shortstop and he's quite good. He hit a double, a single, and a grand-slam homer last Thursday afternoon."

"You were there?" asked Tillie, amazed.

"Certainly not," sniffed the haughty old lady. "Neither my sister nor I care for public affairs; however, his picture was in the paper the next day and I read the account to Ellen."

Tillie and Sigrid headed down the drive to the car, but something made the policewoman look back.

On the porch, Nichole Naughton stood militantly beside her niece, who still wore a troubled expression on her lovely face. A slight movement of the curtain at an upstairs window betrayed the anxious presence of the other sister.

Two reclusive sisters where once there were three, thought Sigrid. Was it possible—?

She opened the car door and Tillie turned the key in the ignition.

"Wait a minute!" Sigrid said sharply.

"Did you forget something?" asked Tillie.

"I'll be right back. You needn't come."

Sigrid walked back to the edge of the porch. Nauman had accused her of cruelty to soft furry creatures, and she knew it would be mean-minded to leave these women in lingering fears.

"It was the annuity, wasn't it?" she asked Ellen Luft. "She knew she was going to die and the annuity would die with her, so she persuaded Dr. Freeman to fake the death certificate and she made your mother take her place, didn't she?"

"Oh, please!" cried Ellen.

"And when Clayton Gladwell came up to talk to Penelope Naughton about her gaudy past, your mother wasn't quick enough to deceive him."

"He was a leech!" said Nichole Naughton fiercely. "All polite and smarmy. 'What's the harm?' he said. 'An innocent deception,' he said. Until Dolly signed Penny's name to the contract. Then he said she could go to jail. That we all could. For conspiracy to defraud. And forgery—even Asa."

"It was what Penny wanted," Ellen said dully. "She was so worried about how we'd survive with no income. She tried to break the annuity, but it couldn't be done even though it was her money. She wrote out a full explanation in case anyone did try to make trouble, and she left all her papers to me. If she'd only lived a few months longer, if the film idea had been brought up before she died, it wouldn't have mattered."

She took a deep breath. "What happens now, Lieutenant?"

"As far as I'm concerned, nothing. This isn't my jurisdiction. As long as you can prove that the four of you were here last Thursday afternoon, I have no reason to pursue earlier events. Goodbye, Mrs. Luft, Miss Naughton."

Ellen Luft's incandescent smile followed Sigrid back down the shade-dappled walk.

"You made her pretty happy," Tillie observed curiously.

"I told them they wouldn't have to worry about being

questioned again." Her tone discouraged further query and they drove silently for a few blocks.

"I sure wish we knew why Gladwell was blackmailing Penny Naughton," he said pensively.

"We can't expect to tie up every loose end," said Sigrid.

Regretfully, she realized that she still didn't know, might never know, exactly why Penny Naughton had left the spotlight almost fifty years ago. Losing the family shoe factory didn't seem like much of a reason to retreat from the city. Nor was an illegitimate child in evidence. Drugs? Alcohol? That didn't fit with the long and vigorous life she had led in seclusion. An unhappy love affair?

Sigrid decided she would have to wait and see the movie. See what Contempo Cinematics came up with.

As they passed Ossining, Tillie turned on the radio to learn if the weather forecasters were still predicting rain soon.

"—and the top story at this hour remains the sensational return of little Jamie Logan!" gushed a network announcer.

CHAPTER XXIII

The news vans and camera crews had departed from outside the Trent townhouse when Sigrid and Tillie pulled up to the curb. A couple of print journalists with more leisurely deadlines had remained to do word sketches of the house and street, and perhaps to catch the servants as they left for the day.

They eyed the two police officers curiously, but further public questioning on the premises was currently limited by a uniformed officer on duty outside the door. He checked their IDs and passed them through to a security guard from Trent's office.

"You've had a hectic afternoon," Sigrid said when Justin Trent joined them in his study.

"The main thing is that it's over," the financier said tiredly. "Now Sarah and Jamie can get away to our place in Westchester. It went well, though."

Sigrid agreed. At headquarters, a television set had been tuned to a local news station when she and Tillie returned from Putnam County, and they had arrived in time for an edited replay of the session.

Trent and his public relations officer, Frank Aldrich, were shown seated in the large formal reception room. Aldrich had read a prepared statement that announced the return of Jamie Logan:

"Of the thousands of children who disappear every year, Jamie was one of the lucky few—a baby taken to replace one that died. We know now that a grief-stricken young woman saw an opportunity to fill her empty arms. She probably didn't know she was going to take Jamie until she was actually walking away from the marina with him.

"Although the woman was unstable, a drug addict and a drifter, she seems to have loved Jamie and provided for him as best she could. He's healthy and well nourished and he has loving memories of his surrogate mother.

"Our private investigation managed to trace them to the West Coast recently, only to find that she had died of a drug overdose a couple of months ago. Since that time Jamie has been cared for by one of the woman's relatives, a person who had no idea who the boy actually was. Blood tests and footprints have confirmed his true identity, and Jamie was restored to his family this past weekend."

("They got lucky there," growled Captain McKinnon, who'd come out of his office to watch the replay. "Most hospitals blur a newborn's footprints until there's nothing on the birth records except a five-toed smudge.")

At that point Aldrich had looked up from his papers and said, "I'm sure you have questions and Mr. Trent and I will do our best to answer. There are, however, two points which we prefer not to discuss at this time: the identity of the woman who allegedly took Jamie and the investigator who found him. There are technical and legal problems still to be resolved, so we ask your understanding and forbearance on these points."

("Good," said Tillie. "We don't need reporters swarming over Gladwell's office yet.")

"To anticipate your most pressing question," Aldrich smiled, "yes, Mrs. Logan and Jamie will be here to speak with you shortly."

A babble of voices broke out, then Justin Trent leaned toward his microphone. "The question was, does Jamie remember his mother or me? I would have to say no. He wants his old blue teddy bear in bed with him at night—that was his favorite toy before he was taken, so we think there may be subconscious memories, but you must remember that he was only a toddler when he last saw us. I'm told that few people retain many memories before the age of two."

"When did you first learn Jamie was still alive?"

"Who was the relative?"

"What led the investigation to the West Coast?"

"What was Mrs. Logan's first reaction?"

"What was his?"

"Was Child Find involved in his recovery?"

"Who brought him back?"

"When?"

"Where?"

"How?"

Trent and Aldrich patiently fielded the questions, answered those they could, smilingly deflected the ones they couldn't or wouldn't. Sigrid noticed that they drew attention away from hard questions by dropping in bits of human interest: Jamie's reaction to an old toy or new book, his eagerness to attend a Mets game, his dismay at getting a complete physical from his former pediatrician.

When the first flood of questions had dwindled into repetition, Sarah Logan and Jamie entered the room quietly and the usually blasé reporters burst into spontaneous applause.

Many of them had covered the original story and remembered her ravaged face—the tremulous mouth begging for her son's return, the eyes sunken and dark-shadowed from nights of sleepless weeping. Most of them knew about the nervous breakdown; two or three even knew about her suicide attempts.

And so they clapped—even the cynics were clapping, in simple pleasure at this happy ending for a radiant Sarah Logan and her small son.

Jamie wore a blue knit shirt and short white pants and he held Sarah's hand tightly. So much light, so many loud cameras flashing and whirring, so many people made him shy and he pressed himself close to her side when she sat down to answer questions.

His shyness made the reporters considerate for once. After Sarah spoke of her great joy, she smiled down at him, cuddled under her arm, and asked if he would tell the people about the new bicycle he and his grandfather were going to pick out soon.

Complete silence fell as the six-year-old whispered into the microphone. Haltingly at first, then gaining confidence, he told how his grandfather said he could have a red bicycle but he wanted a green one with gold racing stripes like a friend he once knew had. Tommy. "And Tommy's bicycle goes two hundred and eighty miles a minute!"

Thirty veteran reporters had hung on every word.

"We appreciated your not mentioning Clayton Gladwell's name," Sigrid told Trent. "It helps not to have reporters muddling the witnesses and second-guessing our investigation."

"I was afraid they'd sensationalize his murder and try to link it to Jamie," Trent admitted. "That's why I wouldn't give the name of the relative who kept Jamie after that woman died. It sounded logical to say she was still grieving and didn't want any publicity."

"Does that mean Rachel Elsner *isn't* grieving?"

"I forgot, you haven't met her yet, have you, Lieutenant?"

"That's one reason for our coming this afternoon. But if Miss Elsner doesn't regret her sister's death, I'm surprised she isn't out selling her story to the press."

In her years on the force, Sigrid had seen friends or relatives of the newly dead reveal their most intimate secrets to the media for money. She said as much to Trent.

He nodded ruefully. "I know. Fortunately, Miss Elsner has a strong streak of respectability. She's afraid if her church friends found out, she'd suffer guilt by association. Just to be safe, though, Aldrich and three of my lawyers put the fear of the Lord into her this morning—part carrot, part stick. She's signed a contract. Twenty-five thousand a year for five years' silence. We promised we'd sue the socks off her, put her *under* a prison, if she even whispered the names of her sister or Jamie."

"What about your servants?" asked Tillie.

"That's always a possibility, of course," Trent said. "But they've all been with us a long time without capitalizing on it. Miss Elsner has had little contact with them. And anyhow, we've arranged for her to fly back to California around midnight tonight."

He paused courteously. "Unless you object, of course. She's had no direct contact with Clayton Gladwell, you understand."

"Still, we do want to see her," said Sigrid. "First, though, to get back to Gladwell's death, did you know Dave Shovener?"

"Shovener?" Trent repeated thoughtfully. "No, I don't believe—wait. Did he work for Gladwell? I'm not sure. Clay Gladwell liked to keep the details of his operation confidential, but a few months back he said one of his private detectives was on a very strong trail. If I'm not mistaken, he referred to that detective as Dave. Is that correct?"

"It is."

"But he's not the one who found Jamie," said Trent. "That man's name is Bailey Dunne."

"Dunne was the detective who finally traced him to California, but it was Dave Shovener who first came up with Evelyn Elsner's name," Sigrid said.

"Gladwell seems unable to have kept any investigator for very long and he and Shovener parted company about three months ago. Among Gladwell's secret accounts we found that he paid a 'D.S.' twenty-five thousand around that time. In cash. It was listed as a first payment. Did that money come from you?"

"I really don't know," said Trent. "I told Gladwell to spend as much money as it took to find my grandson. How he rewarded his employees was his business. I suggest you ask Mr. Shovener."

"We can't," Sigrid told him. "He was killed in Chicago a couple of months ago."

"What do you mean? An accident? Murder? How?"

Sigrid nodded to Tillie, who had collated all the information Chicago had sent to them that afternoon through the wonders of modern telecommunication.

"The Chicago police assumed that Shovener was shot during an ordinary break-in," Tillie said. "He was killed with a .22 bullet. So was Gladwell. Microscopic comparisons of the two bullets would indicate that they came from the same gun."

"*My* gun was a .22," said Trent, turning to Sigrid. "You're not accusing—"

"No, sir. It's a different gun."

"Then I'm sorry, Lieutenant. I just don't see how this relates to me at all. If Shovener died before he found Jamie and if Clay was shot with the same gun, doesn't that indicate the killer is someone connected with another matter altogether? An earlier client perhaps? The other evening you spoke of blackmail. Maybe Shovener uncovered something criminal about one of Gladwell's clients and was blackmailing him. You said a lot of Clay's records were burned. How will you ever know for sure?"

"We may not," Sigrid conceded, "but we have to check everything we can. And that includes asking Miss Elsner if she did meet Shovener."

"As you wish, Lieutenant Harald. I'll have someone show you to her room."

Rachel Elsner had been given a comfortable suite on the top floor.

"It's almost like an apartment with room service," she told Sigrid and Tillie. "Bedroom, sitting room, even a little kitchen."

She folded back a louvered screen to reveal a tiny alcove fitted with a sink, hot plate and under-the-counter refrigerator.

"The Trents have been real nice, invited me to eat downstairs with them; but most of the time I nibbled on something up here. The maid brings me anything I want. I'm going to miss this back home."

Rachel Elsner had a plain weathered face. She might have been prettier as a girl, but at thirty, time had begun to pinch her. Her mouth was discontented and there were frown lines in her forehead and between her eyes. The robe she wore looked new, perhaps bought for this trip east, but it was a nondescript beige. A navy blue shirtwaist hung waiting on the closet door. All her other possessions were neatly packed in the open suitcase on the bed.

She held a Bible in her hand, but she had been watching a giggle-and-jiggle sit-com with disapproving voyeurism when the two police officers entered and she still gave the television partial attention.

"May I?" said Sigrid and reached over firmly to turn it off. "We'll only bother you a few minutes, Miss Elsner. You've heard about the death of Clayton Gladwell?"

"The lawyer that got Mr. Dunne to find Mike—I mean, Jamie? Yes, they told me he got shot Thursday night. I talked to him over the phone once, but I never met him . . . is he writing down everything I say?"

Tillie smiled at her reassuringly. "Not every word, Miss Elsner. Just enough so I can remember what's been said."

"We gather your sister's son—her *real* son—was born in the New York area," said Sigrid. "Had you ever seen him? Did you know he'd died?"

Miss Elsner shook her head. "My father threw Evvie out when she was sixteen, after he caught her with the McDonald's manager back home in South Dakota. He gave her a good belting the first couple of times. The last time, he packed up all her clothes and dumped them on Chester Thornton's front doorstep. That's the McDonald's manager. He had a wife and three little girls, so he bought her a ticket to New York and put her on the next bus.

"It was three years or more before she came back. Daddy'd died by that time and I'd moved out to California with one of my church friends. We thought it'd be nice not to mess with shoveling snow again. Mary—that's my friend—she got homesick and moved back pretty quick, but there's a Pentecostal Holiness Church of Jesus only two blocks from my apartment and I had a pretty good job, so I stayed.

"Anyhow, when Evvie went home, Mary gave her my address and she wrote me. Sent me a picture of her and the baby. She had the nerve to ask for part of the money from the house just like she'd been there and helped with Daddy's last days instead of whoring off to New York, winding up with a baby and no husband.

"Here," she said, riffling through the pages of her Bible. "Here's the snapshot she sent."

The photograph had been taken in bright sunshine and was overexposed, but the plump girl who laughed into the camera bore a strong resemblance to Rachel Elsner. Her hair seemed to have been bleached nearly white and her eyes were mascaraed into dark blotches; but in the picture, Evelyn had possessed a sassy prettiness her stringier sister lacked. Her ripe figure had been crammed into tight jeans and T-shirt and the baby straddled one hip.

He squinted into the sunlight and it was impossible to guess his age or make out distinct features—only chubby legs and arms and a head of blond curls.

"Did you answer her letter?" asked Sigrid, passing the picture to Tillie.

"I sent her four hundred dollars. That seemed like a fair share considering she hadn't been there to help. The house didn't bring very much anyhow."

"When did you next hear from her?"

"About three and a half years ago. She and the boy showed up at my apartment. I let them stay a couple of nights, but I could tell Evvie hadn't changed her ways. In fact, she'd got worse—liquor and smoking that dope; then she started pestering me that she didn't get all the inheritance she deserved. I gave her another three hundred, but I told her straight out that was all she was ever getting and not to come around anymore. I'd have died to have any of my friends see her like that and have to tell them she was my sister.

"And that's the last time I saw either of them until the police called and told me she was dead and to come do something about her and the kid. Five hundred dollars it cost to get her cremated."

"And she never gave you any indication that her real son had died back east?"

"Not really."

"But there was something?" Tillie suggested.

She nodded. "When Evvie first came out, she said she'd brought Mike out to California because it was healthier there. She said Mike had been awfully sick—in the hospital even. She said he almost died. And then she'd hug him and hug him, over and over.

"I told Evvie she was going to spoil him with all that hugging. Always brushing his hair and singing to him if he cried. It wasn't natural. Spare the rod and spoil the child, Daddy always said. And it's true," she told them, clutching her Bible tightly. "He never whipped her like he did me till he caught her with Chester Thornton, and look how she turned out!"

Sigrid had a sudden bleak vision of what the Elsner household must have been like.

Despite Clayton Gladwell's crimes and misdeeds and even granting that he'd been paid for his services, the murdered lawyer at least deserved praise for delivering Jamie Logan from the dominion of this woman.

She kept her voice pleasant, though, and asked, "Before your sister died, did you or she meet a man named Dave Shovener?"

"I told you—I hadn't seen or talked to Evvie in three and a half years." Rachel Elsner pursed her thin lips. "I don't know who she was sleeping with."

"Yet Bailey Dunne reported that when he contacted you two weeks ago, you didn't seem surprised to hear that your nephew might be someone else's child. How was that?"

"Just that nothing she did ever surprised me."

Rachel Elsner suddenly found it difficult to return the other woman's steady gaze.

The Bible said if thy right eye offend thee to pluck it out and she couldn't have made Evvie stop taking drugs, so there was no call to feel blame. Evvie'd always got around men, even Daddy would have taken her back, kept calling for her at the end. That man should have helped her. Instead of calling up a good Christian woman in the middle of the night.

"Are you Evvie Elsner's sister?" he'd asked; when she'd said she was, he'd said, "Lady, you ought to do something about her and the kid. She's spaced out half the time and the kid's not eating right. Even if he's not really your nephew, you ought to do something."

"What do you mean not my nephew?" she'd asked.

"Ah, hell, you know what I mean. She was on a crying jag last week so I hadda listen to all that crap about how her own baby died and how this kid belonged to a friend who didn't want him no more. But even if he's no kin to you, I'm telling you, lady, you ought not to leave him with her."

"It's nothing to do with me," she'd said. "Call the police if you're so worried."

And then, two days later it was the police calling her, saying come and get the kid. It wasn't her fault Evvie'd died, and it wasn't because she felt she'd been wrong not to go earlier that she had taken Mike, but because it was her Christian duty to give him a Godly home.

But she couldn't tell all that to this Lieutenant Harald, who was looking at her like she wouldn't understand how if you tried to pick up dirt, you'd get dirty yourself.

"I just never felt like he was blood kin," said Rachel Elsner. "I don't know why."

The glance Sigrid shared with Tillie confirmed their impression that the woman was holding something back, but they couldn't budge her.

Later, inching their way back downtown in streets clogged with the rush hour traffic of late afternoon, they finally decided that Evelyn Elsner must have let something slip about stealing a stranger's child and that sister Rachel was afraid she'd be in trouble if she admitted she'd known earlier.

After eight each night the staff of the Lantana Walk Nursing Home was sharply reduced—a registered nurse and aide on each of the two floors, an orderly somewhere asleep but on call if needed.

By ten o'clock most of the rooms were dark except for an occasional bluish glow where someone had fallen asleep in the middle of a program or where some night owl whiled away the passing hours of darkness. The lights in the hall had been dimmed. Only the nurse's station at the intersection of the two wings was normally lit.

Elaine Albee looked up from her magazine as Blanche Rhodes returned from a coffee break with the other nurse downstairs.

After twenty years of running her feet off at the Downstate Medical Center in Brooklyn, Mrs. Rhodes was quite satisfied with the prospect of working here until retirement. It might not pay as well, but it was a shorter commute and easier work. She was not sanguine about Quentzl's replacement, though. Too young and too pretty to last long here, she thought.

Mrs. Rhodes had seen too many cuties zip in and out to think this one would be staying, for all the interest she showed and all the questions she asked about how the place was run. "Two dollars says she doesn't last six weeks," she'd told Hazel Stone over their coffee just now.

"No takers," an equally cynical Hazel had said.

Elaine Albee glanced at her watch as Mrs. Rhodes appeared. If Mrs. Rhodes's idea of a coffee break was only ten minutes, it would be hard to leave the floor long enough to examine the master files that must be in Burchlow's office. Three minutes had been ample time to flip through the records here at the desk and see that they contained only day-to-day medication data on each resident; gaining access to the complete records was going to be trickier.

"That was a short coffee break," she said pleasantly.

"Mrs. Stone had to leave," said Mrs. Rhodes. "One of her patients jerked his I.V. out."

The first floor held only half as many beds as the second, but they were occupied by the more seriously ill, the patients in need of constant medical attention. Already, Elaine Albee had learned that residents of the second floor equated a move to the first as an admission of terminal illness even though Mrs. Rhodes assured her that was not always the case.

"Mr. Scocozza was down there eight weeks last year while they got his heart regulated and now he's back up here again."

The nurse glanced down both halls in case there was a call light glowing, then settled herself behind the counter and picked up her crocheting.

"If you want a cup of coffee now, feel free," she said. "In fact, you could stretch out on the couch in the lounge if you like. I'll buzz you when something comes up."

"Thanks," said Albee, "but instead of putting my feet up, do you think it'd be okay if I took a quick run around the grounds? Jogging's more relaxing for me."

"Sure," said Mrs. Rhodes as her crochet hook flashed in and out of the green afghan she was making for her first grandchild. "It's a quiet neighborhood. You shouldn't be bothered. Just don't lock yourself out. Higgins will blast your eardrums if you wake him up for something like that."

"Oh. Is it Higgins on call tonight?"

Mrs. Rhodes heard the misgiving in the younger woman's voice. "Mean-looking devil, isn't he?" she agreed. "I think even Mr. B's a little scared of him. Don't worry. Higgins sleeps like a log. Just stay out of his way and you won't have any trouble with him."

"I'll certainly try," Albee promised.

She slipped down the wide shadowy stairs to the lobby, past the deserted reception desk to the female staff lounge where she made herself a cup of tea. While it steeped, she opened her locker, took out the picklocks and penlight she'd stashed there earlier and put them in her pocket. Then, carrying the Styrofoam cup, she strolled back out into the darkened lobby.

All was quiet.

She stayed close to the wall and edged around the corner of the hall leading to the critical care ward. There was no sign at first of Mrs. Stone or her aide. A few seconds passed, then she saw the aide emerge from a far room with a bundle of bloody linens. Duty and preoccupation were in her movements. With a little luck, both women would be busy for the next fifteen minutes.

She turned back to the lobby, disposed of her cup and went out to the main doors. The lock was a simple push-button affair and she fixed it so that one of the double glass doors could be opened from outside. If Mrs. Rhodes came looking for her, she would assume her truant aide was out jogging around the building.

Although still hot, the night air was inviting, and for

a moment Elaine Albee lingered on the threshold and wished she really could go for a quick run instead of snooping through Burchlow's office.

A sudden uneasiness swept over her and she whirled, half expecting to see someone. The shadowed lobby was silent and empty, but her feeling of being watched remained.

She shrugged off her nervousness and, moving quickly now, hurried around the reception desk to the inky black alcove that led to William Burchlow's office. The door was locked, of course, but it was a simple Yale model and Albee was rather cocky about her expertise with a picklock.

Quietly she pushed open the door and shone her narrow beam across the large inner office. File cabinets lined the wall behind Burchlow's desk.

She closed the door and crossed the thick carpet noiselessly. As she circled Burchlow's desk, she was surprised to see a folder with her name on it. Inside was the form she'd filled out with mostly phony information when she applied for the job earlier in the day.

She wasn't happy to see that it was still unfiled and wondered if Burchlow intended to check her references. No matter. By the time any letters could return from her fictitious jobs in California, she should be long finished here.

"Start with Dussel," Lieutenant Harald had told her. "We're looking for evidence that Gladwell was blackmailing Burchlow. Misuse of his power of attorney, maybe. Looting his inheritance. We don't know, but you'll probably recognize it when you see it."

Albee opened the drawer marked "Current—A–L" and was too absorbed in her task to notice the blocky shape that had been motionless behind the door when she entered.

Holding her penlight steady, she flipped toward the middle of the drawer and there it was, "Dussel, Helmut."

She reached to pull it out and was abruptly wrenched away from behind. Before she could cry out in pain, a thick hand clamped down over her mouth and a raspy voice growled in her ear, "What the hell kind of game you running, girlie?"

Robert McLamb stopped on the third landing of the apartment stairwell on West Twenty-third Street and puffed noisily. God, he was out of shape! Time was, he could have bounded up these steps like a mountain goat.

"Time was, you weren't three years past seventy either," he reminded himself dourly.

Still and all, Dan did it everyday and him only two years younger. Anything Dan Embry could do, he could do, thought McLamb. Hadn't he spent every Monday night for the past twenty years proving it?

He patted the hefty little case tucked inside his jacket pocket, the silver darts Kathleen had given him on their twenty-fifth wedding anniversary, the darts that regularly beat Dan's steel ones down at Madigan's every week.

Only, Dan hadn't shown up tonight and that wasn't like him. They hadn't missed a dozen nights in as many years and, besides, there was his line busy every time he tried to call.

Who was Dan talking to so long that he couldn't stop and call Madigan's if he wasn't coming? Dan's Marie had passed away even before Kathleen and there were no children there.

McLamb topped the final flight of stairs and walked around the corner to Dan Embry's apartment. When he knocked, the door edged open a crack.

"Dan? It's me—Robbie." He pushed the door wider.

The apartment was only an efficiency, so the whole room could be seen from hall lights spilling through the open door.

Dan Embry lay in a pool of dried blood on the sofa, his arm flung across the telephone, which was half off the hook.

Robert McLamb's eyes stung with sudden tears. His first thought was, "No more Monday night dart games"; his second was for his old friend.

"Ah, Dan," he grieved. "Ah, Danny boy."

CHAPTER XXIV

When Sigrid Harald's bedside clock alarmed in the mornings, it could be temporarily silenced by a tap on the top. In five minutes it would ring again, and Sigrid would again grope for the snooze button with sleep-groggy fingers.

This would continue in five-minute intervals until the repetitive motions had eased her gently into the waking world.

On Tuesday, however, she was blasted from her pillow by a two-pronged attack as alarm clock and telephone shrilled simultaneously.

For a dazed moment she stared at the two instruments stupidly, unable to decide if she should answer the clock or tap the telephone. Then the last foggy wisps of sleep cleared from her brain and she tucked the telephone under her ear and shut off the clock.

It was Captain McKinnon.

"I thought you'd want to know," he said brusquely. "They found an old man in an apartment near the Chelsea Hotel last night. Dead at least two days, maybe three. Dan Embry. Looks like he was shot with the same .22 that killed Clayton Gladwell."

• • •

When Sigrid reached her office forty-five minutes later Tillie was there before her, already leafing through the preliminary reports.

According to the uniformed patrol officer who had responded to the call, the door to Embry's apartment did not appear forced nor was the apartment ransacked.

The cheerfully nosy little law clerk had been shot once through the chest. No one seemed to have heard the shot since the occupants of the apartments on either side of Embry's had been away for the weekend. The tenant immediately above Embry was hard of hearing but thought he'd heard a car backfire Saturday morning just after dawn. The woman one flight down and two apartments over said she'd heard a backfire around midnight on Friday.

To add to their problems, the building was not air-conditioned and the July heat made estimates of the time of death just that: educated guesses, nothing more. Sometime between Friday night and Saturday afternoon, the Medical Examiner's office thought, but one could read between the lines and find the M.E.'s palms-up shrug.

From Ballistics came quick confirmation that the slug removed from Daniel Cicero Embry's chest had been fired from the same gun that killed Clayton Gladwell last Thursday and Dave Shovener back in May.

There was a manila envelope with the contents of Embry's pockets at the time he'd been moved: a handkerchief, a roll of digestive mints, a wallet with thirty-six dollars and the picture of a middle-aged woman whose hair and dress suggested the fifties, some loose change, an old-fashioned pocket watch, a ballpoint pen and a small appointment book with the month of July torn out.

By Dan Embry or by his killer?

The pocket watch reminded Sigrid of one her great-uncle had owned. One seldom saw gold with that tinge of rich orange anymore.

The case was so old that parts of the filigree design were worn smooth and Sigrid held it in her hand, remembering her pleasure when Uncle Lars would open the front to show her the slender second hand sweeping across the ivory face with its spiky Roman numerals. More intriguing was to open the back and watch the delicate flywheel shuttle back and forth.

Sigrid looked closer at the open back lid, for she remembered that Uncle Lar's had been a double that concealed a second flat section where he kept a picture of his wife.

She found a hairline crack in the edge of the lid, levered it gently with her fingernail, and as the thin gold leaf swung up, a scrap of paper fell to the desk.

Tillie was at her shoulder as she unfolded the slip of onionskin.

In Dan Embry's minute script were the names H. Dussel, E. Elsner, E. Dorato, and Nellie G. On the back was a lightly penciled phone number and the name Donaldson with a question mark beside it.

"Donaldson?" said Tillie. "Now where have I heard that name?"

Before Sigrid could speculate, there was a tap on her open door and Detective Elaine Albee appeared. Her left cheek was scratched and her eyes were darkly circled as if she hadn't slept, but her pretty face was triumphant as she presented Sigrid with Rick Higgins.

He had traded his orderly's rumpled uniform for a light blue sports jacket and sharply creased slacks, yet he still looked faintly evil.

"He's Secret Service," said Albee, a tinge of awe in her voice. "They're running an undercover operation on Burchlow."

"And on the two doctors connected with Lantana Walk," said Rick Higgins, flipping open his identification for Sigrid to see.

"Social Security call you in?" asked Sigrid.

"That's right," he answered, a little surprised that she'd guessed. "They asked us to investigate the forged endorsements of social security checks. A couple of doctors have been channeling into the home patients who get respectable monthly incomes but who have no nosy relatives to ask questions.

"We haven't seen any evidence of foul play—we'll give

them that—but after those particular patients die, no death certificates are issued until well afterward. And the monthly checks keep getting cashed. We can document over thirty cases so far."

"What about Helmut Dussel?" Sigrid asked.

"Dussel? Oh, yeah. The guy Goldilocks here was interested in. His social security checks go right into Burchlow's pockets. Those trust funds he inherited, too.

"Of course they can make a good case that it's mostly legitimate. That's the beauty of their setup. Health care, custodial care—it's costly. Lantana's lawyers can make a good case for taking all a patient's money while he's living. No way, though, can they get around forging names on checks issued to dead people.

"Anyhow, Lieutenant, we're not ready to close them down yet, so do us a favor and pull Goldilocks out of the place, okay?"

"Detective Albee was there to investigate a murder and possible blackmail," Sigrid said coldly.

"Yeah, she told me. Blackmail I can't help you with; but if you're thinking to hang a Thursday afternoon murder on Burchlow, forget it. He keeps a .45 in his desk, but he didn't leave the nursing home until six that day."

CHAPTER XXV

"You can't milk a dead horse," Uncle Lars used to say, and Sigrid acknowledged this to be one of those times.

"If you'll give Detective Albee a statement describing Burchlow's movements last Thursday, we'll back off," she told the Secret Service agent.

"Too bad," said Tillie when they were alone again. "Burchlow's operation sounds profitable enough to make killing a blackmailer worthwhile."

"I don't know," said Sigrid. "Considering the money the home must be grossing, Gladwell's take seems rather modest. Of course, he may not have guessed the full extent. Perhaps he only stumbled on their greed when Burchlow used his power of attorney to get at Dussel's inheritance.

"At least it shortens your list," she smiled, referring to Tillie's penchant for methodical tabulations.

They looked again at Dan Embry's paper.

"Nellie G. Why Gladwell's cleaning lady?" Tillie wondered.

"And why Elena Dorato?" asked Sigrid. "She's been dead twenty years. And yet— Remember that auction I told you about? Satterthwaite's. Those Cinderella slippers are being sold tomorrow. I think I'll give them a call."

"And I'll call this number," said Tillie, copying down the digits from Embry's list.

Sigrid's call took several minutes to complete, and at the end she was only slightly wiser than when she began. After being shunted upward through Satterthwaite's hierarchy, she finally spoke to the highest on-premise authority and explained her interest in the Cinderella slippers.

"They've been withdrawn by the owner," said authority.

"Who is that?"

"I'm sorry, Lieutenant, but we cannot disclose that information. Our records are kept strictly private."

"But this is a police matter."

"So you say," said authority with a slight sneer. "Anyone can lift a telephone and claim to be a police officer."

"If you doubt my identity," Sigrid said patiently, "look up the number in your phone directory and ask for me, Lieutenant Sigrid Harald."

"I could do that," authority conceded, "but you would be no further. Try to understand, Lieutenant. Our clients are often embarrassed by their need to sell. Were we to betray our trust, we'd soon find ourselves with no consignments. No, the only way we will disclose such confidential information is with a court order."

Tillie was no more successful.

"It's the main number of a hospital up in the Bronx," he reported. "I didn't know what department to ask for so the switchboard connected me with the business office, but they didn't recognize Embry's name or Gladwell's.

"I think I remember, though, where I heard the name Donaldson. Wasn't he the PI who worked for Gladwell before Dave Shovener?"

Sigrid didn't know.

"Shouldn't we take one more look around Gladwell's office now that they've had time to sort things out?" Tillie asked hopefully. "Maybe they know what Embry was up to."

"That's a good idea, but you'd better start without me," she said, looking at the accumulation of papers on her desk. "I'll get through some of this and meet you there around lunchtime."

She spent the next hour and a half diligently reading, sorting, and rerouting her share of departmental paper, but Gladwell's murder was the most interesting of her current cases, and when she could leave the others with good conscience she called a central registry and asked if they had a current listing for a private investigator named Donaldson, first name unknown.

There were three: Scott, Samuel and Leo. The first one she tried, Scott Donaldson, was not her quarry; but he told her he thought Leo had worked for Gladwell a year or so ago.

She started to dial again when she became aware of Detective Peters waiting for her attention just inside her door.

"Lieutenant Harald!" His homely face shone with suppressed excitement. "It's about Dr. Bhattacherjea and that little girl. You're not going to believe this!"

"Try me," she invited.

Too keyed up to sit down, Peters described his interview with the school principal in Brooklyn Heights the day before.

"Mr. Greene made some phone calls and Family Court's involved now. Immigration, too. That little girl— Halima: turns out she's not the Bhattacherjeas' niece. She's their slave!"

"*What?*"

"Honest to God, Lieutenant. They bought her from the kid's mother back in Africa a couple of years ago for two hundred dollars. They make her clean the place, wash and iron, and take care of the three little boys, too."

Peters had just come away from the long and vocal confrontation still going on between Family Court representatives and Immigration on one side and, on the other, the Bhattacherjeas, who were indignant that the blackmail they had paid Gladwell was proving their downfall.

"Even at three hundred a month, they got a bargain while it lasted," said Peters, who had a working wife, two preschool daughters and a perpetually disheveled home. "Do you know what day care and maid service cost these days?"

Peters went away, still shaking his head, and Sigrid returned to her interrupted telephone call.

Happily for her, if not for Leo Donaldson, the private detective was sitting idly by his phone, hoping for a client, when she rang.

"Hey, yeah, I saw that Gladwell caught a bullet," he said cheerfully. "Doesn't surprise me."

"No?"

"Naw. He could be a real pain in the old you-know-what. What's the word I want? Capricious? That was Gladwell—capricious as hell. All buddy-buddy one day, a hard-assed bossman the next. Liked to play games. I never knew what was behind half the things he asked me to do."

"Give me an example."

Donaldson thought a moment. "Okay," he said, "how's this? He sent me down to City Hall one day to look up a parking lot down near the Battery. I had to copy off the names of every owner right back to the Indians practically. And when I gave him the list, he read about halfway through it, smirked like he'd just been given a Christmas present, then tore the paper into a hundred little scraps. Did that make any sense?"

"It might if you found a name that shouldn't have been there," Sigrid said, half to herself.

"How's that?"

"Never mind. Mr. Donaldson, did you do any work for him concerning the kidnapping of Jamie Logan?"

"Not really. I mean, I was there and all when Sarah Logan tried to kill herself the last time, but I didn't come up with anything useful. Was Gladwell still on it? They didn't say on television who did the legwork."

"We'd like it kept confidential for now; but yes, Gladwell's office located the boy."

"I'll be damned!"

"You say you were with Gladwell's office when Mrs. Logan tried to commit suicide—"

"Slashed both wrists," Donaldson put in genially.

Once again, Sigrid thought what a talent Gladwell had possessed for hiring pleasantly stupid people to do his donkey work. Here was another innocent with no idea of the lawyer's penchant for blackmail.

"Would you tell me what you remember about that time?" she asked.

"Sure. Let's see now . . . I went with Gladwell about a year and a half ago. I guess he mentioned he was working for Mr. Trent, but everything had sort of petered out. Gladwell didn't put me on it until after I'd been there a couple of months. That was early spring or late winter a year ago."

Here Donaldson digressed into an argument with himself as to whether it was February or March of the previous year that they'd heard about Sarah Trent Logan's mental breakdown and attempted suicide. Sigrid's pointed questions eased him back to the main track.

"I guess the month's not important," he said. "Anyhow, Trent lit a fire under Gladwell that day. Told him to find his grandson, he didn't care what it cost. They must have been in Gladwell's private office two or three hours going over all the leads.

"After Trent left, Gladwell came up with the idea of having me check out all the charity hospitals in the area for a kid of that description. Told me to look for a transient or hippie-type mother and what would be just one four- or five-year-old Caucasian kid with A-positive blood. He said maybe the sick kid might be the Logan boy. Sounded dumb to me, but what the hell? It was his money."

"Did you have any luck?" asked Sigrid.

"Naw. I busted my butt and got him a list of twelve or fifteen names, but before I could check out any of them, Gladwell started nit-picking my expense account and I quit. Listen, I never padded expenses in my life. Every penny I put down, I spent!"

Sigrid cut through his grievances to ask, "In the list you made for Gladwell, do you recall the name Evelyn or Evvie Elsner? With a child named Mike?"

She could almost hear Leo Donaldson thinking hard over the telephone.

"Nope. Sorry, Lieutenant. I don't think so."

"What about Dave Shovener, the investigator who replaced you?"

"What about him?" asked Donaldson, his breezy voice suddenly cautious.

"Did you know him? Was he competent?"

"I never met him. Heard some talk, though."

"Yes?" Sigrid encouraged.

"He got results, I guess, but the word is that he didn't always play it straight."

"You mean he'd falsify information?"

"That and also, well, I heard he didn't mind roughing people up a little to find out what he wanted to know. They say he got killed out in Chicago. Probably tried to lean too hard on the wrong guy."

"What about Bailey Dunne?"

"Who's he?"

"Gladwell's last PI, the one who finally found the Logan boy."

"Don't know him, but his fortune's made; lucky dog, winding up a big case like that."

Perpetual insolvency sounded in Donaldson's voice.

The Westchester house was one of Sarah Logan's favorite places.

Basically Queen Anne in architectural style, the cottage was a charming sprawl of turreted and gabled roofs, wide shady verandas and a peacefulness that made it seem as if the nineteenth century lingered there, enfolded by towering shade trees and overgrown rhododendrons which swept across the smooth green lawns and shut out the rest of the world.

She and Jim had spent their wedding night there and it was there she had come to get back her strength after Jamie's difficult birth.

The New York townhouse, the villa on Ischia, the apartments in Mexico City, Tokyo, L.A.—those were her father's: beautifully furnished, meticulously staffed extensions of his wealth and power.

The Westchester cottage had been her mother's. It still had most of its original willow and wicker furniture and was staffed by a middle-aged couple who somehow managed to preserve the comfortable homey feeling the house had always held for Sarah.

Around the corner of the house came Mr. Biggins with a long aluminum extension ladder on one shoulder and a brassbound wooden swing over the other. He wore a pair of gray corduroy trousers and a red plaid shirt that Sarah could have sworn was twenty years old. Clamped in his teeth was another of those half-smoked dead cigars which he was never without.

The Bigginses had worked here since her own childhood, but Sarah couldn't recall ever having seen Mr. Biggins actually smoking. She used to creep along the hedges and watch him as he hoed the vegetables or pruned the shrubbery, hoping to catch him in the act of striking a match or with smoke actually curling from the stub. It never happened.

Behind him, laboring with a coil of slender chain that kept sliding from his hands, came Jamie.

"This maple or the oak over there? Which do you think?" Mr. Biggins asked the little boy.

Jamie considered both trees solemnly. "Which do *you* think, Mr. Biggins?"

"Well, your mother had it in the maple when she was your age, but you'll probably want to go higher than she ever did and there's more room around the oak."

"Okay. My friend Tommy, he can stand up and pump. He can make the chain go straight out."

Chattering happily, Jamie followed the big man across the yard as Sarah emerged from the dining room onto the side porch where she was helping Mrs. Biggins set up a table for their lunch.

Her heart turned over at the sight of the small towhaired child beside the burly caretaker. The wonder of his being here was still too new and precious to take for granted yet.

"Oh and it's grand to have the two of you here again," said Mrs. Biggins from the doorway behind her. "Biggins wants to drag out every toy you had as a child. Remember the pony cart?"

"Is that still down at the barn?" cried Sarah, delighted.

"Nothing gets thrown away with Biggins around. I told

him not to count his chickens, but he's sure you'll be wanting another pony for young Jamie."

"It'll make more work," said Sarah, but her eyes had caught the sparkle in Mrs. Biggins's and they laughed together, remembering how Biggins had spoiled the last pony until it was so fat it could hardly fit between the cart shafts.

They spread a cloth over the wicker table and Mrs. Biggins set the two places with silver and rose-sprigged earthenware.

While the housekeeper went back to check on a pan of ginger cookies, Sarah perched on the porch railing and watched Jamie hold the ladder as Mr. Biggins secured the ends of the chain to a high limb. By the time Mrs. Biggins was ready to serve lunch, Jamie had already tried out the swing and came running across the lawn laughing, "Did you see how high I went? I'm going to swing higher than Tommy when I'm that big!"

"Don't get too big too soon," she wanted to say as she helped him wash up; but she held back the words, willing herself to put the old grief behind and live in the present.

Somehow she would find the strength to make last night's outburst her final blast of bitterness and regret.

It had been an effort to summon up a last bit of polite friendliness for Miss Elsner when that woman finally departed for the airport shortly before midnight. All self-conscious smirks, Rachel Elsner kept mixing embarrassed apologies for her dead sister with earnest promises to avoid the media.

"Thank God she's gone!" Sarah had cried.

"A dismal person," Justin Trent agreed, "but she wasn't responsible for her sister's acts."

"I don't care! They were sisters and I'll never forgive either of them for what was done to Jamie and me. *Never!*"

"Sarah," said Trent, startled by the venom in his daughter's voice. "Honey, forget it. The woman's dead now."

"I'm glad she's dead. She deserves it for stealing four years of my son's life from us. I'm sorry if that sounds harsh, Father. I know it's not rational to hate someone so much, but I *do*.

"She took my baby. She left us in limbo. We didn't know if he was dead or alive, loved or sodomized. How can I understand her? Or forgive? *You* don't forgive people who hurt you, and I'm your daughter," she said proudly.

Trent sighed then. "Yes, you learned that from me. It was your mother who always found reasons to excuse. Maybe we should remember her example."

"Turn the other cheek?" Sarah asked scornfully.

"You have Jamie back," he reminded her. "Let the rest go, Sarah. Don't let it make you bitter."

She had gone to him then and put her arms around him, grateful to this good steady man who had always put her first since her mother died—first ahead of business, ahead of everything—who refused to give up on her even after she'd given up herself, who had known that Jamie would come back someday and had made her hang on.

"Thank you for not quitting," she had whispered. "For bringing Jamie back to me."

Now she dropped a light kiss on her son's freshly scrubbed face and her eyes misted when Jamie gave her a spontaneous hug in return.

CHAPTER XXVI

I

When Sigrid joined Tillie at Clayton Gladwell's depleted office that afternoon, she found a shattered Nancy Kuipers.

The office manager's translucent skin was blotched by recent weeping and her clear green eyes alternated between dazed disbelief and numbed anger at Tillie's allegations.

"There has to be some mistake," she pleaded with Sigrid. "Clay a criminal, a common blackmailer? He couldn't have been. I loved him! We were going to marry, Lieutenant. Wouldn't I have known?"

Her anguish made Sigrid awkward. She never quite knew what to say and her inability to comfort always made her more brusquely official.

"The Bhattacherjeas have just admitted that he was blackmailing them," she told Tillie.

"What for?" Mrs. Kuipers cried wildly. "A misplaced birth certificate? Phony vaccination records?"

"Slavery," Sigrid told her coldly. "They were keeping that twelve-year-old child in bondage and Gladwell not only took money for his silence, his paperwork helped them do it."

Nancy Kuipers turned completely white.

Sigrid had often heard that phrase used before, but

this was the first time she'd ever seen someone do it so totally that even her lips lost color.

Tillie jumped to his feet and caught the woman as she fell. Together, he and Sigrid carried her into the lounge next door and eased her onto the couch.

She had begun to come to by then and resisted their offers of water, a soft drink, tea.

"No, nothing," she said. "Really. I'm all right now. It's that—what you said—My daughter is ten. She thought Clay was wonderful. And he loved her . . . or said he did."

Her pretty face was haggard now and her voice was dull. "He said he wanted to adopt her after we were married. Be a real father to her."

"He probably did," Tillie soothed.

Nancy Kuipers drew herself up into a tight curl at the end of the couch, her feet tucked beneath her, her arms clasping her body as if she were chilled. She looked like a little girl herself, forlorn and abandoned; yet even as they watched, something of her former spirit struggled to get through. She brushed off Tillie's comforting pats and looked at Sigrid.

"Did he use me in his blackmail?" she asked harshly.

Sigrid shrugged. "I don't know. Did he?"

The green eyes blanked over as she remembered and tried to analyze.

"Yes—*no!* Oh, God, I don't know! He told me the envelopes of money were just petty cash. He said the blue folders were sentimental favorites. Every time I wondered about them, he'd smile and tease me that women would never be as businesslike as men because they'd never get over their Pandora complex."

"Dan Embry had a long nose," said Sigrid.

"Is that why he's dead? I thought it was a robbery."

"He was shot with the same gun that killed the other two," said Tillie.

"*Two?*"

Tillie glanced sheepishly at Sigrid, but she was unperturbed by his slip.

"Dave Shovener was killed in Chicago a couple of months ago," Sigrid said. "Same gun."

Millicent Barr poked her blond head around the corner of the lounge. "Sorry to interrupt, but—"

She broke off, embarrassed by the tension-charged scene at first; then natural warmth took over.

"Are you all right, Mrs. Kuipers? Something else bad hasn't happened, has it?"

"No, Milly, it's nothing. Just a bit shaky on my feet for a moment. Did you want me?"

"You said to tell you when he came. Bailey Dunne. He's here to clear out his things."

"Thanks, Milly. Ask him to see me, please, before he leaves."

As the girl left, Nancy Kuipers swung her feet to the floor and stood resolutely. "Tell me straight, Lieutenant. Is someone systematically killing everybody in this office?"

"I doubt it," Sigrid answered. "Leo Donaldson worked here before Shovener and he's still alive; Bailey Dunne came afterwards and he seems unthreatened. No, my best guess is that Shovener uncovered something very damaging and your fiancé used it for blackmail. The victim probably shot them both to protect his secret."

"Then Dan Embry stumbled across it and was given the same treatment," said Tillie.

"Poor old Dan. He liked gossip and he could never resist a puzzle. He always had to know why, just for the fun of knowing. That's what made him such a good law clerk. He loved to track down precedents and ramifications." She sighed, then said, "How can I help?"

"For starters, you can check back to when Dave Shovener was here and give us a list of cases he alone worked on," said Sigrid. "Especially the blue-folder cases."

"Anything else?" Nancy Kuipers's face still looked drawn, but her voice was brisk.

Tillie had been examining the office accounts before Sigrid arrived and he had a question.

"It's not really important," he said, "but how is Nellie Goldenweiser paid? I don't see her name on the account books."

"Of course not," said Kuipers. "Maintenance is included in the rent."

"But she's not part of the regular building maintenance," said Tillie. "The doorman told us last Thursday that she was extra, hired by Mr. Gladwell."

"Nonsense. All janitorial services are provided for in the rental lease. If they weren't cleaning properly, it would be my job as office manager to see to it; and I would certainly know if we'd hired someone special."

"She told us she oils the wood furniture and panels, things the night crew doesn't have time for," Tillie argued.

"Leave it for now," Sigrid told him.

Normally Sigrid wasn't bothered by Tillie's habit of getting hung up on minor details, but she could see that his insistence on the cleaning woman's special status was getting Nancy Kuipers upset all over again.

He dropped it, but his round face had lost its usual cheerfulness, and as Tillie walked back to Gladwell's inner office, Sigrid knew she hadn't heard the last of how Nellie Goldenweiser had been paid.

This was the third working day since Gladwell had been shot and his office vandalized. In that short time, order had been almost completely restored.

There was still a large stack of unsorted papers on a chair beside Jean Parrish's desk, but nothing remained on the floors. The secretary's chair had freewheeling castors, and she hitched herself along from one end to the other of the file cabinets banked around her desk. She worked with single-minded perseverance and didn't look up as Sigrid passed.

At the front end of the office, in the small chamber off the main lobby, Bailey Dunne was emptying the contents of his desk and closet into a couple of cardboard boxes. He picked up a manila folder as soon as he recognized Sigrid.

"Hi, Lieutenant. Milly told me you were around. Thought you might like to see this," he said, flashing his toothiest, blue-eyed, all-American grin. "They're the notes Dave gave me on how he traced the Logan boy."

As a working draft, Dave Shovener's notes were very sketchy. Even though he had supposedly been working on the case for eight or nine months at the time, his first entry was dated April of this year.

Of course there was still the probability that he'd been working on something entirely different during those unaccounted-for months. Something that had backfired on both Gladwell and him? Maybe Nancy Kuipers would come up with something.

In the meantime this report began with the bald statement that Evelyn Elsner's son Michael, age two, had died in a South Bronx hospital four summers ago, but no mention of how Shovener had come up with her name or who had fathered the boy.

Hospital records had provided him with the address of a boardinghouse in the Bronx—"bums, whores, and hoboes" was Shovener's cynical appraisal of the tenants. The janitor was uncooperative until a twenty-dollar bill reminded him of Evvie Elsner, whose baby had been so sick with chicken pox and a high fever that she'd taken it to a hospital late one night.

He swore he'd never seen her again, but another twenty helped him remember that she'd mentioned a sister in California who owed her some money.

Shovener had listed various agencies he planned to check for further leads in California, among them the Department of Motor Vehicles, Welfare and AFDC.

"I'll keep this for the time being," Sigrid told Bailey Dunne when she'd finished reading.

"Okay. Too bad Dave wasn't able to stick it out with Gladwell a few months longer. Then he'd be the one getting Trent's big bonus instead of me. And maybe he wouldn't be dead out in Chicago."

Sigrid realized he didn't yet know that the same gun had killed both his predecessor and their employer.

While she hesitated over telling him, Dunne brightened and said, "Embry said he lasted longer than any of us, though. Guess he couldn't beat the law of averages."

"Embry said? When?" she asked sharply.

"Last week sometime when I was moaning about having to find another place. Gladwell had told us that he was retiring and I was sorting my papers, deciding what to keep and what belonged here. Embry said I'd lasted here as long as most PI's. He said Dave held the record, though—almost a year."

"Did Embry see those notes?"

"Gee, I don't know. Maybe. The folder was there on the desk, I guess. He always talked a mile a minute when he was in here. Always flipped through everything, too. He reminded me of the wrens that fly around our porch back home. They poke their bills in the clothespin bag, hop in and out of the firewood, never miss a thing with those little sharp eyes. That was Embry. Damn shame what happened to him. I tell you, New York streets these days—"

"How do you think he died?" Sigrid asked curiously. "Wasn't he mugged?"

"No, Mr. Dunne. He was shot. With a .22."

"Like Gladwell?" His handsome mouth hung slack with surprise.

"Exactly like Gladwell," she told him. "And like your friend Dave Shovener, too."

As Sigrid walked back through the blue-carpeted hallway, she couldn't help remembering four years ago and all the intense effort that had gone into the search for Justin Trent's grandson—the FBI, state patrol, and every spare person in the NYPD.

How had Shovener picked up on a recently bereft mother that an official search had overlooked? He seemed to have earned the twenty-five thousand Gladwell had paid him.

Only, what did the notation in Gladwell's secret account book mean? Why a "first payment" to "D.S." when Dave Shovener had quit?

She drew level with Jean Parrish's office and, on sudden impulse, asked the secretary, "Did you ever type up any reports for Dave Shovener?"

"Sure, Lieutenant, but like I told Mrs. Kuipers, there's nothing in his folder anymore. See?"

She rolled over to the appropriate file drawer and extracted a folder with Shovener's name on it. As she'd said, it was completely empty.

"Maybe it's still in the pile you haven't sorted," Sigrid suggested with fading hope.

"Maybe," Jean Parrish agreed, a placid lack of interest in her cowlike face.

"I guess you don't remember any of his reports about the hospitals he searched, that sort of thing?"

"No."

Sigrid had started to turn away when she heard Jean Parrish say, "Anyhow, was that Dave or Leo?"

"Leo? Leo Donaldson?"

"Uh-huh. When he quit, he left some papers in his office and Milly brought them to me and I put them in his file. I came across them Friday. I *think* they were hospitals."

She waggled her chair along with her plump bottom till she was back at the *D* file. With unhurried motions, she plucked Leo Donaldson's folder from the drawer, looked through the contents, then handed it over to Sigrid.

Only that morning, Leo Donaldson had told her over the telephone that he'd located some twelve or fifteen names that fit Clayton Gladwell's specifications of an unattached transient mother and a blond, blue-eyed child with A-positive blood who had been seriously ill around the time Jamie Logan was kidnapped.

Leo Donaldson was mistaken.

He had found twenty-two possibilities.

Number twenty-one on his list was "Evelyn Elsner/Michael Elsner" and the same South Bronx hospital.

Sigrid continued down the hall, trying to work out how Donaldson's list fit in with Shovener's notes. She wanted to discuss it with Tillie, but when she entered Gladwell's office she found an excited Tillie gathering up papers on his way to find her.

"Look here, Lieutenant!" he said upon seeing her. "I was right about the cleaning woman."

She started to cut him short, but he seemed so pleased and eager with whatever he'd found that she hadn't the heart to squelch him. Patiently she sat down at Gladwell's desk and watched Tillie open the blue folder devoted to Elena Dorato.

"I almost missed it," he beamed and handed her photocopies of the *Golden Princess*'s crew and staff at the time Elena Dorato had jumped from one of her decks. The list began with the captain and continued on down through the ranks for several pages. There must have been a thousand names.

"Next to last page," Tillie said helpfully.

Sigrid turned to it and there, tucked neatly among the laundry maids, was the name Nellie Goldenweiser.

"That's not all," crowed Tillie, thrusting another document into her hands.

It was a copy of the actress's will. Half her large estate had gone to an actors' relief fund and a retirement home; the other half had bought annuities of various amounts for a couple of dozen dressers, secretaries, maids, housekeepers and cooks. Among them—surprise, surprise—was Nellie Goldenweiser.

CHAPTER XXVII

There was no way of judging in exact dollars and cents how much Nellie had profited by Elena Dorato's death, because the annuities had been distributed as shares. Half Dorato's estate was to be held in trust, with the yearly income divided into twenty-five parts. Two of her beneficiaries were to receive three parts of the interest, five would receive two parts, and nine more received one part each.

Nellie was one of those receiving two parts.

Tillie punched some numbers into the calculator on Gladwell's desk.

"If Elena Dorato left a million dollars to the trust fund and it was invested at eight percent, Nellie could be getting over six thousand a year," he said. "That doesn't sound like much now, but it was enough for one person to live on twenty years ago. That would make a pretty good motive for murder."

"So you don't think Dorato committed suicide?"

"You always say you don't like coincidences," he reminded her. "Here's somebody who worked for Dorato, who was down in her will for two shares of a trust fund, and who just happened to sign on for the same voyage where Elena Dorato died. That's an awfully big coincidence, Lieutenant."

"Gladwell must have thought so too," she mused, turning the blue folder in her hands.

"That has to be why Nellie's not carried on his office accounts."

"Payment in kind," Sigrid nodded, remembering the notation written beside Elena Dorato's initials in Clayton Gladwell's secret ledger.

With single-minded intensity, Tillie was ready to hop over to Brooklyn and tackle Nellie Goldenweiser right then. Sigrid brought him back to earth.

"Nellie may have been capable of pushing an actress over a ship rail," she said, "and perhaps Gladwell could have goaded her into killing him; but Dave Shovener out in Chicago? Or Dan Embry?"

"Her name was on Embry's list," said Tillie, but he reluctantly conceded that interviewing the cleaning woman could wait until they had finished the tasks at hand.

Sigrid showed him the list of names the secretary had given her from Leo Donaldson's file, and followed it with the précis Dave Shovener had given Bailey Dunne.

"That's the same hospital that Embry had a phone number for," said Tillie. "More coincidences?"

Sigrid reached for the telephone and dialed the digits Tillie read off to her. When the hospital answered, she asked for the records department, identified herself and requested confirmation that a Michael Elsner, infant, had died there four years previously.

"What's going on?" asked the clerk. "I told someone from the police just last week that no Michael Elsner died here. Don't you people talk to each other?"

"Last week? Are you sure?"

"Let's see . . . it was Friday. Around four. A Detective Somebody-or-other. Wilson?"

"Detective Tildon?" asked Sigrid.

"Maybe. I don't remember the name. I looked up the kid's records though and told him what we had. Michael Elsner was treated for a high fever and severe dehydration—chicken pox complications, y'know?—and then released a couple of days later. You want me to pull the record again?"

"Please," said Sigrid. "We'd like to know his blood type and the attending physician."

"Hold on," sighed the clerk.

While she waited, Sigrid told Tillie, "Someone called them Friday afternoon pretending to be you."

"Dan Embry?"

"Probably. He had the number, Bailey Dunne said Embry probably saw Shovener's notes, and we know he was helping Mrs. Parrish sort papers Friday morning. He could have seen—"

She broke off as the hospital clerk returned to the other end of the wire.

"There was no personal physician," said the clerk. "Welfare clients usually see whoever's on duty at the time."

Sigrid listened, jotted down the dates and the names of the two pediatricians who'd attended the Elsner child, and then thanked the clerk.

"A-positive blood," she told Tillie.

"But the dates are wrong," he objected. "This kid was out of the hospital before Jamie Logan was kidnapped."

"Maybe he had a sudden relapse," said Sigrid, whose knowledge of childhood diseases was, at best, extremely dim.

Tillie snorted. "Of chicken pox?"

Three of his four children had itched their way through the disease at the same time. Shelly still carried a small pockmark on her right cheek like a nearly invisible beauty spot. The kids had been uncomfortable, and he and Marian had been run ragged for a couple of weeks; but once they started getting over it, recuperation had been rapid and Tillie said as much to Sigrid.

"Well, we know he died of something," Sigrid said impatiently.

"I'll check for his death certificate," Tillie said.

While he called the Health Department, Sigrid wandered down to Nancy Kuipers's office.

Bailey Dunne was with the auburn-haired office manager. He had just handed over his keys to the office and received his final check. Sigrid didn't ask the amount, but from Dunne's gosh-gee-whiz grin as he left, the bonus he'd earned for finding Jamie Logan was quite generous.

"Were you able to isolate Dave Shovener's cases?" Sigrid asked her.

"Not completely. Jean hasn't found any of his reports yet. They must have been destroyed. I've Xeroxed our running expenses for that period, though, and you can see that most of his items are charged to Justin Trent's account. There doesn't seem to be much that he worked on alone and nothing else that was blue-folder."

Sigrid looked through the pages. Dave Shovener had become Gladwell's resident private investigator a year ago the past June.

"Clay and Leo Donaldson had argued over Leo's expenses and Leo quit," explained Nancy Kuipers. "Then Dave came in and picked up where Leo left off. You see, Leo had compiled a list of possible women who might have taken Jamie, and Clay wanted Dave to check them all. There were quite a few names—nearly two dozen, I think—all transient types, and in three years they had scattered all over the place, from Canada to Florida."

She ticked off the passing months with motel bills from Alabama, airline tickets to Toronto, a rental car in Wisconsin.

"Clay got impatient. He thought Dave was dragging his feet, and Mr. Trent was pressuring them both. Anyhow, he and Dave had a rather loud fight in April and he fired Dave outright."

Tillie had joined them as Nancy Kuipers described Dave Shovener's dramatic storming from Gladwell's office, and he was looking over Sigrid's shoulder when Kuipers noted that she'd drawn a check to cover Shovener's final salary on the eleventh of April.

"Beach Nut Motel," he read. "Laguna Beach, California? I thought Shovener didn't go to California—that it was Dunne who followed up the leads out there."

"Oh, no. Dave was there several days before Clay called him back." Mrs. Kuipers consulted another folder and produced the telephone bill for the month of April. There was a collect call from Sacramento on the third of

April, and two from Laguna Beach on the sixth and seventh.

On the morning of the eighth, Clayton Gladwell had called Shovener and ordered him back to New York.

"It doesn't make sense," said Sigrid. "He was so close to finding the boy. Laguna Beach is just south of L.A."

"That's the way Clay was." Mrs. Kuipers hesitated, trying to find the right words to describe the dead man's dual nature. "He was patient and considerate of our regular office staff. Never lost his temper if someone made a mistake. Always remembered our birthdays with flowers or a little gift. But somehow he couldn't seem to get along with the investigators. I don't know if it was because he missed fieldwork and felt confined here—if that made him resent the men who were out there . . ."

She turned up her hands in graceful defeat. "Whatever the reason, every six months or so they'd rub each other the wrong way or something, and then the detective would quit or Clay would fire him."

"Convenient," said Sigrid as she and Tillie drove back to headquarters.

"What?" asked Tillie, easing their car between two yellow cabs at the stoplight. The air conditioning on this particular car was working at less than half strength, but since the street temperature was well over ninety, they had the windows closed.

Sigrid blotted perspiration from her forehead and yearned for a cool swim. The airless car felt gritty and claustrophobic. She tried to ignore it.

"Convenient the way Gladwell kept the links of information cut," she said. "I have a feeling that every time his detectives uncovered something solid—even if Gladwell couldn't use it as blackmail right then—they were eased out as soon as he could manage it.

"Look at Donaldson. He came up with a list of potential kidnappers, then Gladwell goaded him into quitting.

"Shovener had a solid lead on her and he was fired.

"Bailey Dunne actually found her and he also found that the Bhattacherjea child was not at the school she was supposed to be enrolled in. How long do you suppose

Dunne would have lasted if Gladwell had decided not to retire?"

"Shovener doesn't seem to have picked up anything of blackmail value," said Tillie.

"Nancy Kuipers didn't recognize anything," Sigrid amended. "Don't forget that she told us that very first day that she didn't know much about the blue folders. Something Leo Donaldson said makes me think he provided Gladwell with blackmail information on someone's real estate deals. Donaldson's another of those slightly stupid, incurious gophers like Jean Parrish and Bailey Dunne, who did the work without realizing its significance. He doesn't give Shovener much of a character reference, though."

"Milly Barr either," said Tillie. "She was afraid of him. Said he had dead eyes. There was nothing stupid about him, though, and she was glad when Gladwell fired him."

"What does she think of Bailey Dunne?"

"He reminds her of one of those cardboard cutouts that stand in front of toothpaste displays," Tillie grinned. "Just about as deep, too, she says."

Sigrid was obscurely pleased to hear that the young English girl had not fallen for Dunne's boyish charms. She wondered whether it was native good sense or the pilot at Global, who, incidentally, had confirmed Milly's alibi for the time of Gladwell's death the preceding Thursday night.

"What about records on the Elsner child's death?"

"I'm supposed to call back at three-thirty," Tillie said.

He swerved to miss a delivery truck that impulsively committed a right turn from the left lane ahead of him, and they drove the rest of the way absorbed in separate trains of thought.

At three-forty a puzzled Tillie reported to Sigrid in her office.

"It's crazy," he said. "The Health Department has never issued a death certificate in this city for any infant named Michael Elsner. Shovener lied to Dunne about that."

Sigrid leaned back in her chair, her gray eyes thoughtful. "Assume Michael is still alive, Tillie, and where does that leave us?"

"You mean Jamie Logan is really Michael Elsner?" he asked. "You think maybe Gladwell decided that after four years any little blond-headed kid with the right blood type stood a good chance of being passed off as the Logan boy?"

"Why not? He could control comparisons of a prospect's footprints with those on Jamie's birth records. Those hospital footprints are usually worthless anyhow. All Gladwell would need is a transient mother and a suitable boy," said Sigrid, continuing that line of thought. "Donaldson got him a good list of possibles and then Shovener started checking them out. Maybe the first twenty had the wrong physical looks or too many family connections."

"And on the twenty-first, he gets lucky with Evelyn Elsner!" exclaimed Tillie. "She dies of an overdose and the kid lands with an aunt who doesn't even want him."

"Another coincidence?" said Sigrid. "I don't believe it."

She looked again at their copy of Gladwell's long-distance telephone calls. "When exactly did Evelyn Elsner die and where?" she asked.

Tillie pawed frantically through his notes, went back to his own desk and soon returned with hard facts: Evelyn Elsner's body had been discovered on the eighth of April in a shack outside Laguna Beach. "She had been dead at least a day."

"With the telephone wires busy between Gladwell and Shovener," said Sigrid. "Query California and ask if there's any chance someone helped Evvie to an overdose. After all, Shovener came back to New York for a very dramatic firing on the eleventh of April and on the twelfth, Gladwell secretly handed him $25,000."

"Hey, that's right," said Tillie. "I forgot about Gladwell's ledger. 'First payment.' Do you suppose Gladwell shot Shovener to keep him from telling Trent that his grandson was a fake?"

"If so, who shot Gladwell? Or Dan Embry?"

"Trent?" asked Tillie dubiously.

"That doesn't sound logical, either," sighed Sigrid. "Trent might *sue* Clayton Gladwell for fraud if he thought the lawyer was foisting off a phony grandson on him, but kill him? Before the child even arrived? We must be missing something."

She sat at her desk for some time after Tillie had gone for the day, trying to make some sense of the sequence.

Captin McKinnon paused in her doorway on his way out. "Any progress on the Gladwell homicide?" he asked.

Sigrid gave him a condensed rundown of their findings and McKinnon's eyes narrowed when she described their discovery that the real Jamie Logan might still be missing.

"You mean that little kid they showed Sunday night's a ringer?" he growled.

"He could be."

"Could be's not good enough, Harald," he told her flatly. "You'd better be a hundred percent sure before you open that can of worms. Looked to me like Trent and his daughter were both pretty positive he was their kid."

"After four years, how can they be sure?" she argued. "Babies all look alike."

"Not to their mothers," said McKinnon.

"No? Every year there's at least one story in the paper about some mother going home from the hospital with the wrong infant."

It was the first time she'd really argued with him and McKinnon was surprised to notice that there was something of Leif Harald, too, in the flash of her eyes, the thrust of her chin. He clamped down ruthlessly on the memories stirred by the younger woman's face.

"This isn't a newborn infant we're talking about," he said harshly. "This is a baby they held every day for two years. If Justin Trent says it's his grandson, if his daughter says it's her son, you'd better have damn good proof he *isn't* Jamie Logan before you stir up more grief for those people."

He stomped from her office, leaving Sigrid angry and

frustrated. In the time that she had worked for him, she had never seen him buckle to money and power.

She pushed away from her desk in sudden distaste. Enough was enough for one day.

CHAPTER XXVIII

Outside, the air felt heavy and foreboding and a haze over the afternoon sun only intensified the sultry glare.

Sigrid moved aimlessly along with the homeward-bound crowds, but halfway down the subway stairs the jammed trains and stagnant air seemed so repugnant that she fought her way back to street level, flagged a passing cab and gave him the crosstown address of her favorite spa.

By six o'clock she was slicing through cool clear water.

Others had succumbed to the same impulse, unfortunately, and the pool was too crowded for mental letting-go. She was forced to give her attention to the lanes on either side as well as to the other two people in her own lane, trying to avoid their flailing elbows, hoping not to misplace an arm or leg of her own. Eventually, though, the pool cleared out until she had a lane to herself. She stroked cleanly and mindlessly then, giving herself up to the pleasure of the water.

After nearly half an hour, when she was almost too tired to continue, she felt the familiar rush of wind as her lungs seemed to deepen, almost as if her body were a car that had slipped into overdrive. Each time it happened, she felt as if she could swim forever.

The water sluiced away the day's tensions, and when

she flipped over onto her back to begin cooling down, she was relaxed enough to admit to herself that she'd overreacted to McKinnon's words.

Quite rationally, he had merely told her to be sure of her facts before speaking out about Jamie Logan. He had not said she couldn't speak if she had proof.

The therapeutic lift of her swim carried over through the evening. She faced Roman Tramegra's tuna-in-aspic salad with equanimity and was rewarded by a homemade lemon pie that was pleasantly tart.

Roman was in high spirits. "I think—only *think*, mind you—that we may have the solution to our housing problems," he told her.

More explicit he would not be. "I don't want to raise your hopes too high, my dear, in case they are dashed again."

That was as close as he could bring himself to mentioning the collapsed apartment at Schnitzler's bakery.

But he could not resist happy little smiles at the thought of his current plans, and he kept beaming at Sigrid until she retreated to her room early with a book.

At nine, he tapped at her door hesitantly. "If you're too tired to come out again, I *quite* understand," he assured her, "but did you remember that they're showing *Cinderella* tonight?"

It was a happy reminder—exactly what she was in the mood for. She had already unbraided her hair and changed into a pale yellow nightgown with narrow straps, but she followed Roman out to the living room and curled up on the white linen couch. Her dark hair spilled over bare shoulders and gave a softness to the strong lines of her face.

They were just in time for the opening credits, and soon Elena Dorato's golden voice was heard among the enormous pots and pans in a grim stone kitchen. Dressed in rags, a smudge on her nose, the girl scrubbed and rinsed and the pots banged in cheerful counterpoint to her song. A soap bubble floated up to the shadowy rafters and burst beside the cartoon animation of a drowsy silvery spider.

The silver spider, of course, would soon be revealed as Cinderella's fairy godmother.

It had been years since Sigrid had seen the film, but it held up and was still as enchanting as ever—naïve and innocent in a way films may never be again.

Even though she knew what was coming, Sigrid could laugh again at the antics of the two old-time vaudevillians who played the ugly but conceited stepsisters, and feel a renewed sense of wonder as six cartoon mice pirouetted across a real marble balustrade behind the king's musicians.

The glass slippers held an added interest for her now, and her eyes were on them every time they appeared.

During one of the commercials she told Roman, "I called Satterthwaite's and asked about the slippers, but they've been withdrawn from sale and no one would tell me who owned them."

"I *do* hope he's a movie buff with a shoe fetish," said Tramegra.

"Someone who once worked for Dorato is more likely," she said.

"Roman, have you ever heard of a woman named Nellie Goldenweiser?"

"Goldenweiser?" He turned the name in his mind, but for once that storehouse of trivia was barren. "Who's she?"

"A cleaning woman who lives in Brooklyn now, but she's listed in Elena Dorato's will as a housekeeper and she was a laundry maid on the ship when Dorato supposedly jumped."

"Really? And she owns the slippers?"

"We're not sure."

"What a fascinating article that might make for *Movie Magic* magazine," he said. "*Do* find out."

"We intend to," she promised and settled back as the commercial ended and the film resumed.

When the Lord High Chamberlain, played by a wildly funny Billy De Wolfe, knelt at the feet of the ugly stepsisters, Roman said, "See, my dear? That shoe he's holding isn't as long as his hand."

By the time the camera was ready to linger on Cinderella's bare feet, viewers were so prepared for daintiness that they did not notice that the shoes were now more than twice as long as before.

Roman sighed as prince and scullery maid rode off into the moonlight and the fairy godmother transformed herself back into a drowsy silver spider. He switched off the television and said, "Such a pity to lose so much beauty before her summer days were spent."

Sigrid smiled at his fanciful choice of words, but they set up an echo in her mind and she pulled a poetry anthology off the shelf as she passed and carried it to bed with her.

With two pillows propped behind her back, she turned through the pages, lingering over favorite passages, until she found the lines she wanted from a Yeats poem—a poem that rued time's transmutation of his lover's passionate intensity into domestic wisdom:

> . . . O she had not these ways
> When all wild summer was in her gaze.

She switched off her bedside lamp and had just slipped under the sheet when the skies outside arced with bright jagged flashes of lightning. Thunder overrode the sounds of traffic, and within minutes heavy rain sheeted the city.

Sigrid got up again, turned off the air conditioner and opened her windows wide. Normally indifferent to weather and to nature in general, she welcomed the breaking of the heat wave and breathed in the smell of cool, rain-washed air.

All night she dreamed of Cinderella, scrub buckets, and clear, rushing water. Inexplicably, the fairy godmother had turned into Jack Frost and the glass slippers were made of ice.

CHAPTER XXIX

There was a freshness in the July morning that made summer in the city seemed almost halcyon as Sigrid and Tillie drove through streets that were still puddled with last night's rain.

Instead of the Battery Tunnel, which was faster, Tillie opted for the venerable and beautiful Brooklyn Bridge. A cloudless blue sky made every strand of its steel cables stand out in crisp relief, and the East River far below sparkled and gleamed like a tourist office's retouched photographs.

It was a day for dawdling, and Tillie kept taking right-branching roads until they were on the Belt Parkway, skirting the western shoreline of Brooklyn, right under the huge Verrazano Bridge, just past Fort Hamilton to Bensonhurst.

Tillie and his family had watched *Cinderella* too, and he was half whistling a bouncy rendition of "You're Beautiful," the syncopated, self-congratulatory duet of the ugly stepsisters, when they pulled up at the address Nellie Goldenweiser had given them last Thursday night. Tillie had expected a shabby one- or two-room walk-up in a decaying neighborhood. Instead they found a comfortable two-family brick house set on a small corner lot.

The cleaning woman was in her small front yard, re-

staking a gladiolus made top-heavy by the rain; she re-
garded them dourly as they got out of the car. She
remembered them both, though, and led them around
the side of the house to an enclosed terrace outside her
back door, where a table and a chaise lounge stood in
the shade of a pear tree.

Either rents were much cheaper in Brooklyn or cleaning and polishing must pay more than she'd guessed,
thought Sigrid. Or was life made comfortably middle-
class by her inheritance from Dorato?

"I'll get more chairs," said Nellie in her husky voice.

She brushed aside Tillie's offer to help and walked
heavily up the stoop in carpet slippers that were run
down at the heel. Soon two folding chairs were passed
out.

At the lieutenant's nod, Tillie began telling Miss Goldenweiser what they had learned in the last week; how
they knew now that she had worked for Clayton Gladwell
without pay, that she had been a crew member on Elena
Dorato's suicide voyage and that she'd been a beneficiary
under the actress's will.

The charwoman leaned back in the lounge chair as
Tillie spoke, lit a cigarette from the fresh pack on the
table, and gazed up into the pear tree without comment.

Sigrid studied her blurred profile, her coarse salt-
and-pepper hair, her lumpy figure, and rawboned,
grass-stained hands.

"Why was Gladwell blackmailing you, Miss Goldenweiser?" she asked.

"For the same reason you're here asking that question," she said leadenly. "He thought I killed Elena."

"Did you?"

Nellie Goldenweiser heaved her solid body upright.
She faced Sigrid levelly, and her hoarse voice was urgent.

"On anything you want me to swear, Lieutenant, I
swear to you that Elena Dorato killed herself that night!"

"Tell us about it," Sigrid said.

"I met her out in Los Angeles about four years before
she died. I was housekeeper for a man who owned a
cottage at the beach."

"Laguna Beach?" asked Tillie.

"Laguna? No. That's south of L.A. We were north. On Malibu. Anyhow, my employer leased the cottage to Elena Dorato for a couple of years and she asked me to stay on."

"And did you?"

"Sure. A job's a job, isn't it? Women are usually fussier about things than men, but we got along fine. She was already past her prime then, you know. She'd had a couple of polyps removed from her vocal cords and she was drinking too much and getting puffy around the edges, but she was nice to me. No airs. She called me Nellie and told me to call her Elena. I liked her okay and I guess she must have liked me, to leave me something in her will like that.

"When her lease was up, she moved to Glendale and I decided I'd had it with California. I was tired of palm trees that never changed color in the autumn. I wanted to see snowfalls again instead of mudslides, and I never did get used to earthquakes. Give me New York anytime."

"Did you keep in touch after you came east?"

Nellie snorted and lit another cigarette. "She was nice to work for, but she was my boss, already, not my sister. All I knew about her was what I read in the gossip columns. Sure, I heard she was going to Italy to make a new movie, but it didn't mean anything to me. You could have knocked me over with a feather when I signed up to work that cruise and found she was booked on the same ship."

"A complete coincidence?" said Tillie with a significant look at Sigrid.

Nellie's shoulders slumped.

"Sure. That's what Gladwell said. 'You think the police are gonna buy that, Nellie?' he said. 'You knew she'd left you enough to retire on,' he said. 'Motive and opportunity,' he said."

Sigrid had never heard Clayton Gladwell speak, of course, but the charwoman conveyed a vibrant picture of opportunistic taunts that echoed Nichole Naughton's version.

"Did you meet with Dorato at all on the ship?" she asked.

"Once. We were four nights out from New York. She'd sent some of her lingerie to the laundry and I brought it back to her. She did a real double-take when she saw it was me. At first I thought she was going to high-hat me, but then she pulled me in and poured me a drink and acted like it was old home week. She'd been drinking and she looked like hell warmed over.

"'Takes me two hours every night to put myself together enough to go on deck,' she told me."

Nellie's voice softened as she described that strange evening in the actress's cabin.

Dorato had been drinking heavily but she seemed in control of herself, and her hands were steady as she touched up the roots of her golden hair. She told Nellie that she knew she was on the down elevator, that her looks were going fast and that she was tired of dieting and holding her stomach in all the time.

"Soon it'll be face-lifts and gauze filters on the cameras," she had said, looking at her still lovely face in the mirror.

"No one really cares about me," she had told Nellie. "Oh, it was wonderful at the beginning. Glamorous! All that money and people telling me I was the most exquisite creature since Mary Pickford . . . but they don't care about *me*, Nellie. They just want to be around a movie star, any movie star. You've been my best friend, you and people like you—my dressers and hair stylists and cooks and housekeepers. At least you were honest about our relationship. *Quid pro quo*, Nellie. You did an honest day's work and took an honest day's pay and didn't try to flatter me!"

She had gripped Nellie by the shoulders then with a terrible intensity and demanded to know if Nellie had bragged about knowing her to any of her fellow maids.

Nellie swore that she hadn't.

"Good. Promise me that you won't, Nellie. It's important. *No matter what happens*, you mustn't tell anybody on this ship that you know me. Promise!"

Slightly scared by now and more than a little offended

that Elena didn't want to publicize their onetime acquaintance, Nellie had promised.

"And that was the night she did it," Nellie said.

"Yet even after she was dead, you didn't come forward?"

"I made a promise. Later, when I heard that she'd left me money, I realized that was why she wanted me to keep quiet. She was afraid I'd be accused."

"How did Gladwell find out?" asked Sigrid.

"Who knows? One day, out of the blue, about ten years after Elena died, he called me up, said he knew I'd benefitted from Elena's death and that I'd been on the same ship when she died, so he wanted to talk to me."

Nellie's voice turned bitter. "I knew what he wanted as soon as I heard his oily voice. It didn't take us long to come to terms. I gave him all the cash I had—five thousand dollars—and I told him that was it. I needed the income I was getting from Elena's trust to live on. He said he'd keep quiet if I'd come and clean in his office a couple of times a month. That it'd be worth it to know he had Elena Dorato's housekeeper—and murderer— oiling the leather and polishing the furniture of his private office.

"He was a *shtupping momzer!*" she said, angrily slipping into profane Yiddish. "He'd sit there and watch me sometimes and he'd hum some of Elena's songs. He knew every one of her movies by heart. And sometimes he'd read poems that made fun of me."

Sigrid watched her broad face with an odd feeling of déjà vu. There was something about the woman's eyes, the way she wanted to see how the two of them were taking her words . . . and not only those eyes, but the tilt of her head and the gesture of her hands.

Any other morning and the quarter might not have dropped. So soon after last night, though, after *Cinderella* and after leafing through the poetry anthology, and her odd dream—

"Of course," Sigrid blurted. "Not Jack Frost—*Robert* Frost! *Provide!*"

Tillie was startled, but Nellie Goldenweiser only made a wry, fatalistic shrug of her shoulders.

"So, Lieutenant? Poetry, too, you read?" she asked in perfect Jewish Brooklynese. "Such educated cops we got these days. Just like Mister Clayton-*shtupping*-Gladwell, *nu*?"

She looked at Sigrid mockingly, then she lay back in the lounge chair again. Her voice lost its husky street smarts and became almost golden as she spoke the opening lines of Robert Frost's cynical poem:

> *"The witch that came (the withered hag)*
> *To wash the steps with pail and rag*
> *Was once the beauty Abishag,*
> *The picture pride of Hollywood ..."*

"Elena Dorato?" gasped Tillie.

"Born Eleanor Goldenweiser. Over in Newark."

"But they always said you were Italian," he protested. "You were orphaned when Mussolini came to power."

"You believe studio publicity?" Sourly, she gestured toward the Verrazano looming in the distance. "How would you like to buy a bridge? I can let you have it cheap."

Tillie flushed a bright red.

"How much of that scenario you just gave us was true?" Sigrid asked sternly.

"Most of it. The reasons for wanting to stop being Dorato. I was sick of people sucking up to her, people who wouldn't have given Nellie the time of day. The spotlights were fading anyhow; it was just a matter of time. I didn't want writers and photographers coming round the rest of my life taking pictures of a size eighteen *chotchke* to run next to pictures of me when I was young and pretty. Movie stars are supposed to freeze in time. Get a few wrinkles, add thirty pounds and they cluck about how you've come down in the world. Who needs it?"

"So you staged your phony suicide and sat back and watched the fun?" said Sigrid.

"And don't think it wasn't," Nellie said sardonically.

"Those testimonials at my memorial service, those magazine articles about my inner torments and why I was driven to destroy myself! I wanted to go to the reading of the will, but I decided I probably wouldn't have been able to fool some of my old friends. My real friends."

"Did Gladwell ever suspect who you were?"

"Not at first. I really don't think he did, but he was a sneaky bastard and not a bad actor himself. Sometimes I'd think he knew and then I was sure he didn't. But when he read that Frost poem last year, I knew he'd been stringing me along like a yo-yo."

Tillie was totally bewildered. "So why did you keep going to his office?"

Nellie Goldenweiser gave a sheepish shrug.

"At first I thought it was so I could find the papers he had on me. Then later, when I realized that he really did think I was broke and living on just that annuity . . . well, it was fun. I wouldn't want the whole world to know Dorato's still alive; but yes, it was fun getting dressed up like a charwoman and shlepping over to New York to oil the leather. He was my last fan. Audience of one, but an audience just the same. He was a bastard, though. I was going to have to sell the glass slippers to raise enough cash for his final payoff, but you know something?

"I'm going to miss him."

CHAPTER XXX

Tillie spoke little on their return to Manhattan. He had thought they were about to uncover a dramatic, unsuspected murder from the past, and while the true status of the situation was interesting, when all the dust settled, what had they accomplished? Nothing, he decided.

Ethics must ensure Nellie Goldenweiser's secret, since she was obviously not responsible for the shootings of Gladwell, Shovener and Embry, and she had broken no important laws.

Sigrid was quiet, too, reflecting on the ironic contrasts in this case:

The world assumed that Naughty Penny Naughton was growing old peacefully in upstate New York. In reality, she had been dead and in her sister's grave for over two years.

Elena Dorato was a known suicide. Memorial services had been conducted for her twenty years earlier, her estate divided a dozen different ways; yet Elena Dorato, a.k.a. Nellie Goldenweiser, was alive and well and living in Bensonhurst, of all places.

Little Jamie Logan, kidnapped and feared dead, was newly returned. Supposedly he'd been taken to replace a dead child, Michael Elsner. Now it seemed that Michael was alive and the authentic Jamie still lost.

"The way things are going," Sigrid thought bitterly, "the Bhattacherjeas will turn out to be the girl's slaves and Helmut Dussel will be an ex-Nazi who plans to revitalize the Third Reich with social security pensions."

Back at headquarters, she found a message on her desk from Roman instructing her to meet him at one o'clock at an address on the West Side.

She crumpled the message slip in a momentary flash of irritation, even though it was unfair to blame him for her impending homelessness. He was doing his best for her, tiresome though it was to keep looking at new apartments.

Penitently she retrieved the message slip from the wastebasket, smoothed it out and put it in her wallet.

For the next half hour, she reread the first reports of the two crime scenes as written by the officers who had originally responded to the homicide calls on Gladwell and Embry. Sometimes one could overlook the most obvious things.

Next came a sheaf of technical reports, everything from ballistics to pathology, fingerprints and arson. If an obvious answer was there, she couldn't see it.

The check on gun permits revealed that the usual percentage were exercising their constitutional right to bear arms. In addition to Burchlow's .45 and Trent's innocent .22, Howard Tachs had a permit to keep a .357 Magnum at his gallery, and the Naughton household up in Dowling was protected by a pearl-handled .38 registered to Penelope Naughton.

In his methodical thoroughness, Tillie had inquired about permits issued to Gladwell's three last detectives. Shovener had owned a .357, but nothing was registered for Donaldson or Dunne. The gun in Gladwell's apartment was a .44. Nancy Kuipers said she had never seen one in Gladwell's private office.

Sigrid put aside the reports and wandered out to the squad room where she found Tillie in the corner with a couple of portable chalkboards, trying to integrate a chronology of Gladwell's known blackmail activities with his search for Jamie Logan. It reminded Sigrid of diagraming complex-compound sentences in seventh-grade English classes, an ordeal for others but strangely satisfying for her.

She stayed to watch and contributed her own suggestions. Together, they soon filled both boards.

Using Gladwell's secret ledgers, they began with the blackmailing of an as-yet-unknown some seventeen years ago and ended with Bhattacherjeas, who had been added at the beginning of June.

Over that list they superimposed the employment dates of Gladwell's private investigators, and the pattern they had suspected sprang into relief: a new set of initials had been added to the blackmail roster almost immediately after each P.I. left. Clearly Gladwell had used them to dig out compromising information and then severed their connections with his office so there would be little chance of the detectives' stumbling onto his private shakedowns.

They also noticed that Gladwell had followed the hiring pattern Dan Embry postulated—"Those who care don't know," the law clerk had told them. "Those who know don't care."

Jean Parrish, Leo Donaldson, Bailey Dunne. All were amiable and capable enough employees, but with a singular lack of curiosity about where their assignments fit into an overall picture.

And Dave Shovener?

In his ten-month tenure, no new names had been added to Gladwell's secret ledger.

"But if he was smarter than the rest, Shovener might have tumbled to what was going on," Tillie said. "Maybe he even hit on one of Gladwell's extortion victims and got himself killed that way."

"And the killer then waited two months to shoot Gladwell?" asked Sigrid.

"When Gladwell started calling in final payments in exchange for the stuff in those blue folders, maybe when he got to Shovener's killer, he guessed what had happened and let it show."

"But do you think he even realized Shovener was

dead?" asked Sigrid. "Remember that cross and question mark beside Shovener's initials?"

"Yeah, but even so—" Tillie argued.

If he was right, Sigrid told him, it would mean going back through all the office account books, trying to match initials to names, and then countless interviews with people who currently wouldn't want to admit they'd ever been blackmailed.

Tillie sighed at the thought of all that work.

"A policeman's lot," said Sigrid, with a half smile.

"Yeah," he said glumly.

They turned back to the chalkboards and drew up a second schedule on the Jamie Logan case, beginning sixteen months ago when, according to Leo Donaldson, Sarah Logan had tried to slash her wrists and Justin Trent had lit a fire under Gladwell. Donaldson had compiled a lengthy list of women and baby boys whose profiles fit Gladwell's specifications: unattached women whose blond, blue-eyed, A-positive sons had been hospitalized around the time Jamie had disappeared.

Thirteen months ago Trent had paid Gladwell $75,000 on account, Donaldson had been goaded into quitting, and Dave Shovener had been hired to follow up on Donaldson's names.

In ten months he had eliminated twenty of the twenty-two names on the list, which brought him up to Evelyn Elsner, where the diagrams and timetables began to get even more interesting.

When Sigrid and Tillie finished, the chalkboard read:

3 April—Shovener in Sacramento

6, 7, 8 April—Shovener in Laguna Beach

7 April—Evelyn Elsner dies of "overdose" at Laguna Beach

11 April—Shovener back in NYC, "fired" by Gladwell

12 April—Gladwell gives Shovener $25,000 "first payment"

15 April—Bailey Dunne hired

10 May—Shovener killed with .22 in Chicago

27 June—Dunne finds Rachel Elsner and child in L.A.

The conclusion seemed inescapable:

By April, Shovener was scraping the barrel on Donaldson's list and here was a perfect child. Only a drifting, drug-prone Evvie Elsner stood between him and the huge bonus he'd get for finding a millionaire's cherished grandson, and long-distance telephone bills placed him in Laguna Beach the same day the young mother died of an overdose.

Given Dave Shovener's reputation and assuming that two plus two still made four, Shovener had killed Evvie Elsner and, to dissociate himself from her too-convenient death, had returned to New York for a public firing followed by a private down payment on a hefty reward.

His papers had been turned over to Bailey Dunne with everything except a big X-marks-the-spot. Dunne had almost been led by the hand, yet it had taken him over two months to locate the boy in Los Angeles.

"It must have been frustrating for Gladwell," said Sigrid, "sitting back east here. He knew where the boy was, yet he had to wait until Dunne worked it out on his fingers."

"Do you think Trent knew?" asked Tillie, who was worried by the dwindling number of obvious suspects.

They considered it pro and con.

Sigrid described the way Trent had spoken Saturday night of his daughter's grief, and Tillie agreed that Trent had started pushing harder after her suicide attempt.

"Maybe Trent felt he had to give her a child, *any* child, to keep her from killing herself."

"But would a man like Justin Trent do that?" Sigrid wondered. "He seems to place an almost biblical importance on blood relationships and lineage. As long as there was a chance his real grandson could be found, I just don't believe Trent would deliberately abandon the search for him."

"Gladwell and Shovener were bent enough to try to fool him," said Tillie. "Maybe he killed them for it."

"Before the boy even arrived? He wouldn't have known back in May, when Shovener was killed. Anyhow, Tillie, there's another possibility."

"What's that?"

"Shovener might have muddled the place Michael Elsner died." Sigrid glanced at her watch. It was time to leave and meet Roman. "Why don't you check the death records in Trenton and Hartford just in case this *is* the real Jamie Logan?"

It was starting to get hot again. A Turkish-bath steaminess displaced the morning's freshness as the torrid July sun vaporized what was left of last night's rain. It had been a false lull in the heat wave, not a true break.

Sigrid stopped at a sandwich stand and ordered two pastramis to go, then took a cab to the address Roman had left for her.

Eventually the cab turned into one of those seemingly deserted side streets on the western edge of Greenwich Village right next to the Hudson River. A narrow street that ran straight down to the old abandoned piers, it was lined with small warehouses and other unattractive brick buildings, and she thought at first that whoever had taken Roman's message must have copied down the wrong address. The four- and five-story buildings were so bare of architectural adornment that the street looked as if all the buildings had turned their backs to it, as if one should walk around to the next block to see main entrances, marble cornices, more inviting façades.

"Forty-two and a half?" asked the cabbie, creeping along at five miles an hour.

"That's what I was told."

Abruptly the cab swerved in to the curb before a dark green wooden door set in a solid, plain brick wall. The tarnished brass numbers beside an inconspicuous bell read 42½.

Sigrid paid the driver and got out.

The wall was approximately twelve feet high and, except for the green door, presented no break in either direction. Only the tops of two small trees protruded over it.

She rang the bell and was answered almost immediately by an exuberant Roman Tramegra. His large soft frame filled the doorway, then he pulled her through into a weedy, overgrown garden courtyard.

There was a small broken fountain on one side, some scraggly blue and white flowers in the unkept borders along the outer wall, and a slatted redwood bench under a central dogwood tree.

"Isn't it sheer heaven?" cried Roman, who fancied himself a naturalist. "Don't you love it? Your own private oasis in the middle of Manhattan's concrete desert."

Sigrid had never been caught up in any back-to-nature movement, and several disastrous experiences with potted geraniums given by well-meaning friends had left her with no illusions about the greenness of her thumbs.

If Roman thought she was going to take a place that demanded a gardener—then she remembered: most people thought gardens were desirable; most gardens cost a small fortune. Ergo, this place was well out of her range.

"Roman, why are we here? I can't afford a ground-floor garden apartment."

"Come and look before you decide," he coaxed.

The front door opened directly into a vestibule between the dining and living rooms, where several pieces of large furniture were draped in dustcloths.

Straight down the hall were two large bedrooms, each with its own bath and capacious closets. Around the corner from the main entrance were the kitchen and a service entrance to the courtyard, almost like a private house.

Except for that impractical garden, it really was a perfect size.

There were narrow clerestory windows in the bedrooms, and the other rooms received light from long windows opening onto the courtyard. Even with the dusty drapes and carpets, the rooms were potentially bright and inviting.

"What's back there?" she asked of the hallway beyond the kitchen.

"Maid's quarters and laundry," Roman admitted.

She nodded. "Of course. Maid's quarters. The butler and gardener can sleep out, but what *shall* I do about the coachman?"

Roman was offended. "Really, my dear, sarcasm doesn't become you."—

"Then explain how you think I can live in a place like this."

But Roman wasn't yet ready to come to that point.

"That bag you're carrying emits a wondrous aroma of delicatessen," he hinted. "I brought some frozen yogurt for our dessert."

They ate the pastrami sandwiches on the bench under the dogwood tree, and Sigrid agreed that it was pleasant.

She was not an enthusiastic picnicker, having never seen the point of ants and wasps and gritty food, but Nauman liked to fill a basket and go somewhere drafty and exposed to eat. At least this was more comfortable and private. He would probably like this courtyard, she reflected.

The top floor of the building across the street did overlook the garden, but the buildings on this side had their upper windows bricked or painted over.

"It belongs to my godmother's sister," said Roman.

Sigrid's attention took an immediate detour. She tried to picture Roman as a soft, plump, boneless baby in a long white christening dress.

Roman seldom dropped any reference to his childhood or background. She had the impression that his family were movers and shakers in Cleveland or Minneapolis or some such city—for Sigrid, as for most New Yorkers, America's heartland began immediately west of the Hudson and extended in a fuzzy haze to California where details sharpened again.

She also gathered that Roman's family were of rigid and upright standards and that his mild deviation from the norm was the cause of such scandal and deep shame that a modest early inheritance had been arranged to keep him away from Cleveland.

Or Minneapolis.

Wherever.

"Your godmother's sister owns the apartment?"

"The whole building. It's a sweatshop or printing company or something. There's a slight mechanical rumble at times. Rather like a restful waterfall in the distance, nothing to disturb. Besides," he added practically, "you'll be gone most of the time they're working.

"Tante Ophélie brought me here for tea two years ago. Caroline, that's her sister, remarried shortly afterwards—her fourth or fifth, and at her age! They live in Belgium now, but she's kept the apartment here in case the marriage doesn't work. That's the French in her. The French are dreadfully pragmatic, don't you think? Where they get their reputation for romance I *cannot* fathom."

"So how much rent does the pragmatic Caroline ask?"

"Tante Ophélie acts as her agent," said Roman. He tucked the last morsel of pastrami into his mouth and swallowed neatly. "The total rent is only a bit more than you'd have paid the Schnitzlers."

"Total?" Sigrid stopped in mid-chew. "Is there a catch in this?"

Roman looked embarrassed.

"As you see, my dear, Caroline left several heirlooms here. She did not intend to rent it. All was to be left in readiness."

"In case her marriage failed."

"Exactly. But it hasn't. So now my godmother thinks she would not be averse to receiving some income for it."

Again he hesitated.

"I have to live here too," he confessed at last.

"What?"

"It's the only way Tante Ophélie will rent it. I *told* her you were a police officer, but she's simply *adamant*. She won't trust Caroline's furniture to anyone else but me. Most of it will fit into the maid's quarters and it does have a separate entrance so we would only overlap in the kitchen and garden and really, my dear, you've never shown a passion for either. We've managed very nicely these past two months, have we not? Here I should be underfoot even less."

He smoothed a strand of light brown hair over the high dome of his head and said with sudden dignity, "I should, of course, pay a third of the rent and utilities."

• • •

Privacy and solitude were very important to Sigrid, but in truth, Roman had infringed on them very little. Part of her acceptance, though, had been in knowing his presence was only temporary. If she rented this place, the arrangement would become more permanent.

She thought of Roman's outlandish recipes, his diverting bits and pieces of esoteric facts, his tactful way of disappearing when she wanted to be alone. Moreover, the avuncular affection he seemed to feel for her had been strangely warming at times.

"I suppose we could try it," she said cautiously.

"My dear, *dear* Sigrid!" he beamed. "I assure you it will work out splendidly. I'll make all the arrangements for moving. You needn't worry about a *thing*."

He plunged into the kitchen and returned bearing cups of half-melted blueberry yogurt.

"So pedestrian," he boomed. "These should really be silver beakers of champagne to toast our new venture."

Despite the dappled shade of the dogwood tree, the July sun quickly turned the yogurt runny. The pragmatic Caroline had taken all her flatware except some pickle forks and a couple of narrow iced-tea spoons; and for all Sigrid's care, a clump of blueberries plopped onto the leg of her beige slacks.

"No more laundromats," Roman caroled as he brought a damp cloth to sponge away the juice. "We have our own washer and dryer now."

Her pant leg dried with a slight stain.

"It's barely visible," Roman assured her. "Don't worry. Half Manhattan's walking around with worse. This is summer. Things drip in summer. Just be grateful you aren't wearing white silk."

Sigrid was startled.

"So *that's* what's bothered me all this time," she thought.

From blueberries, Roman diverged to fruit and vegetable dyes used by the Pilgrim settlers, but Sigrid was following logic's straight path at last and she didn't hear him.

"I'm sorry, Roman," she said. "I have to leave. Now."

•   •   •

Her long strides quickly covered the two blocks to a main thoroughfare where she found a telephone. She called Tillie first and told him what to query Westchester for; then she called a local television news station.

CHAPTER XXXI

"Ordinarily, these tapes would be stored in our vaults uptown and you'd have to get an appointment," said the young man. He was the television station's assistant librarian and he obligingly located the cassette Sigrid wanted to view and put it on the player for her.

The newsfilm was exactly as she had remembered it, and Sigrid asked the librarian to note down the tape's retrieval number.

"For the subpoena," she told him.

Tillie was waiting for her when she left the TV station.

"Your hunch was right on the nose," he said as he held the car door open for her.

The butler tapped discreetly at the study door and Justin Trent put his hand over the telephone. "Yes?"

"Lieutenant Harald and Detective Tildon, sir."

"Ask them in," he directed and spoke into the phone indulgently. "Or you could call him Ol' Paint or even Hey You Horse!"

His lips twitched as Jamie gurgled with laughter on the other end of the line.

Sigrid and Tillie were shown in. Trent waved them to chairs and wound up his call.

"I have to go now, Jamie. Tell Mommy I'll call back later."

The financier was casually dressed in chinos and knit shirt and was more relaxed than Sigrid had yet seen him.

"What can I do for you, Lieutenant?" he smiled. "Have you learned who killed Gladwell yet?"

"We hope so," she said quietly. "Mr. Trent, according to the sheriff's office up in Westchester County, you are registered as owning a .22 pistol for your house there. The serial number is different from the one you gave me Friday. Can you tell us the present location of that gun?"

Trent's smile faded. "That's right," he said slowly. "There *was* a gun up there. I forget the caliber, though."

".22," Sigrid repeated.

He shook his head. "I'm sorry, Lieutenant, I just don't recall seeing it in years. Is it important?"

"Three people connected with the search for your grandson have been killed with an unidentified .22. Yes, Mr. Trent, it *is* important."

"I think I'd like a little clarification," said Trent. His eyes hardened as he sat back in his chair. "You sound on the edge of jumping to some rather rash conclusions."

"We don't think so."

Unemotionally, almost coldly, Sigrid laid out the facts they had uncovered.

"We think you paid huge sums of money to Clayton Gladwell to find a substitute child your daughter could accept as her missing son. We know that Michael Elsner did not die four years ago as Shovener said he did, and we're rather certain that your money probably paid Shovener to kill Evelyn Elsner, the boy's true mother.

"Shovener himself is dead now, killed with the same .22 that shot Gladwell and Dan Embry, and you are missing a .22. If we were to check all the airlines, or the log to your private jet, would we find that you were in Chicago on the tenth of May?"

Trent was silent.

"Gladwell would have to be killed to ensure his silence. Shovener, I suppose, had tried to up the ante on his own? And then there was nosy little Dan Embry, who couldn't resist poking into the contradictions."

"If you wish to make serious allegations, perhaps I should have my lawyers here," said Trent. "They will tell you that my business interests often take me to Chicago."

He slammed his hand flat upon the polished desk top.

"Good lord, Lieutenant! You're accusing me of deliberately taking a cuckoo's egg into my nest!" he said hotly. "Would I quit the search for my grandson, knowing he's still out there somewhere?"

"No," Sigrid said. Her gray eyes were compassionate. "No, the only way you'd do that is if you knew all along that he was dead."

Justin Trent returned her gaze steadily.

"You took the boy out in an unfamiliar speedboat, lost control, and he fell overboard and drowned, didn't he? You couldn't admit that you'd let your grandson die by your own negligence, so you faked a kidnapping and let us run around in circles looking for a child who no longer existed."

"It's not true! I left him alone to make a phone call and someone took him."

"No, Mr. Trent." Her voice was implacable. "I don't know much about children, but I do know what happens when a chocolate bar is eaten in a hot car on a hot summer day. The white leather interior of your Cadillac wouldn't have been in such pristine condition if a two-year-old child had been left there with chocolate."

"There'd be smears all over," said Tillie, the voice of paternal experience.

"Am I under arrest?"

"Yes," Sigrid said and Tillie began to read him his rights under the Miranda ruling.

Trent listened courteously until Tillie had finished. "Will your accusations about Jamie be publicized?"

"You are an important man, Mr. Trent," she said. "As soon as the press realizes we've arrested you, speculations will run rampant. One of the networks or newspapers will probably duplicate our investigations."

"My daughter is not strong," he said. It was not a plea,

merely a statement of fact. "That's why I . . . That's why when Jamie . . ."

Even then he couldn't make himself speak directly of his grandson's drowning four years earlier.

"Her husband had just died. She wasn't strong enough to handle another death. It seemed kinder to let her hope."

Trent looked at Sigrid and the ghost of an ironic smile played around his lips. "I remembered you the first day you came. Childe Harold to the dark tower came. I knew you were intelligent."

Tillie looked uneasy.

"Will it bring any of them back to blast Sarah's joy or to return the boy to that appalling aunt of his?"

"Until three months ago, he had a mother who loved him," said Sigrid.

Trent studied their faces, sighed and stood up. "May I call my daughter first? I don't want her to hear of this on a news bulletin."

"Very well," said Sigrid.

"If you've no objection, I'll go upstairs to change and call her from my bedroom. I suppose I may call my lawyer, too?"

"There's no need to change," Sigrid said mildly. "But if you wish to speak to your daughter privately, Detective Tildon and I will wait outside this room."

They stood in the marble vestibule with its exquisite fifteenth-century paintings and spoke in hushed tones.

"It's a shame about the kid," said Tillie. "He's the real loser in all this."

Sigrid thought of Nancy Kuipers and Dan Embry and of Evvie Elsner, whom she'd only seen in an overexposed photograph. Rachel Elsner's jealousy and unforgiving envy of her younger sister had been obvious, and it was too much to hope that she wouldn't vent that resentment on Evvie's son.

It was not going to be easy to live with the knowledge that she was responsible for taking a six-year-old child from a woman who now loved and cherished him, only to give him to a woman who most assuredly would not.

· · ·

At the end of ten minutes they tapped on the study door, opened it and immediately halted at what they saw.

Justin Trent sat at his desk with that same ironic smile as before. "Come in, please, and close the door," he said.

There were two sheets of closely written papers on the desk before him.

To the casual glance, he appeared to have both his elbows propped on the desk with his head resting on his hands. A closer look and they saw the pistol pressed up under his chin, his right thumb on the trigger.

"You wanted my second .22," he said. "Here it is."

"Now, Mr. Trent," said Tillie reproachfully. "This is no way to do."

"Please don't come any closer," said Trent, adjusting the gun. "I should hate to leave without an explanation."

"You mustn't do this," said Sigrid. "Think of your daughter."

"I *am* thinking of Sarah!" he said harshly. "But I'm not a lawyer, so tell me: is it true that deathbed confessions are considered true statements of fact in a court of law?"

"They usually carry great weight," Sigrid conceded.

"I've written it out, and I've made it as plausible as I can with such little time. It's a confession of how and why I killed those three men—Gladwell, Shovener and Embry. There were some stock manipulations last year—there's no way now that it can be proved that I didn't use illegal inside information. I've written that Shovener and Gladwell had documentary proof that I'd committed a crime and that I killed them to stop their blackmail. I've also said that Dan Embry figured it out and that I killed him, too.

"This is my deathbed confession, Lieutenant Harald. That's all you need, isn't it? I could hire the best lawyers in the country and I bet they could get me off with less than five years, but it would destroy Sarah."

"Mr. Trent—"

"An eye for an eye," he said. "If I pay with my life, you won't wreck Sarah and Jamie's, will you?"

"Put down the gun, Mr. Trent," Sigrid urged. "There are other solutions."

"I don't think so," said Justin Trent, and pulled the trigger.

ABOUT THE AUTHOR

MARGARET MARON lives with her artist husband on their family farm near Raleigh, North Carolina. She is a former president of Sisters in Crime.